EVERY WHICH WAY BUT LOOSE

Philo examined himself in the mirror above the sink. The cut in his forehead looked angry. Gingerly he wiped the congealed blood on a wet paper towel. Dumb sonofabitch oughtn't to have done that, he thought.

Philo walked to the refrigerator and opened a beer. He flicked on the radio: country music blasted out of the speaker. He crossed the highway and headed for the shed, cracking peanuts and discarding shells as he walked. It was dark inside. Philo squinted, adjusting his eyes to the dim light. He looked to the right and left. The shed, as far as he could tell, appeared empty. He squinted again in the gloom.

Suddenly, 150 pounds of orangutan dropped on him from the rafters.

EVERY WHICH WAY BUT LOOSE

Jeremy Joe Kronsberg

A STAR BOOK
published by
the Paperback Division of
W. H. ALLEN & Co. Ltd

A Star Book
Published in 1980
by the Paperback Division of
W. H. Allen & Co. Ltd
A Howard and Wyndham Company
44 Hill Street, London W1X 8LB

First published in Great Britain by
Robert Hale Ltd, 1980

Reproduced, printed and bound in Great Britain by
Hazell Watson & Viney Ltd, Aylesbury, Bucks

ISBN 0 352 30795 1

FOR LYNNIE AND GABE

ONE

The pipe truck was heading north. It rolled past the squat dusty stucco buildings that lined both sides of Lankersheim Boulevard. Small businesses and an occasional house sat forlorn and grey between the car washes and gas stations, beneath the humble of power and telephone lines. It was an area that had been in transition for forty years and would continue to be for forty more.

Philo Beddoe eased the truck past a car-load of young Chicanos low-riding a dented, garishly metal-flaked '67 Chevy. The driver's eyes barely cleared the top of the dashboard. Philo grinned as the young driver immediately accelerated, shooting past him angrily to cut into his lane. Philo braked quickly. The faces in the back seat glared at him balefully through the window as the Chevy slowed to a crawl, forcing Philo to downshift. After a moment, *machismo* satisfied, the driver tromped on it, cutting left across the lane of traffic into a taco stand. Philo shook his head in amusement.

Popping a stick of Juicy Fruit gum into his mouth, Philo hummed to the sounds of the current No. 1 country hit, which came from the portable radio stuffed into a corner of the wind-shield above the dash. Carefully rolling the gum wrapper into a silver ball, he flipped it out the window. It was hot, San Fernando Valley hot, dusty, and acrid with the smell of ozone and exhaust.

Jamming his foot to the floor, Philo accelerated through the yellow light at the Roscoe intersection, weaving between a Cadillac waiting to make a left and a tiny Japanese import that had respectfully stopped for the light. The truck bounced over a pothole as Philo pulled a hard right into the chain-linked fenced yard of Familian Pipe and Supply. The truck bounced again as he gunned it over a speed bump and pulled into an empty slot between two other identical pipe carriers. Grabbing the radio, Philo slapped open the door and slid his 220-pound, 6-foot-4 frame out of the cab.

Several men waved to him as he moved across the yard to the dispatcher's shed. He waved back perfunctorily. Pulling his time card from the rack, Philo slid it into the slot below the clock. The machine clunked morosely. Philo withdrew the card, checked it against the clock, and redeposited it into the rack. Leaning over the counter, he gave the pretty blonde dispatcher a quick kiss. She grimaced, then flashed him a grin. "Delectable," he said.

Making his way back across the yard, Philo climbed into his battered Chevy Apache pickup. The radio popped on, KLAC, "California Countree," filled the cab. Broken hearts, bars, and what's Momma gonna do now that Daddy's gone. He was humming again as he pulled out of the yard, heading on Lankersheim toward Sunland.

The traffic was heavier now, impatient with commuters returning home from their eight-to-fives. Philo threaded his way through the cars, maintaining a steady thirty-five, changing lanes abruptly, scooting past harried housewives and weary salesmen, making each intersection just as the light turned yellow.

Turning right at Tuxford, he pushed the Apache to fifty on the straight stretch to Sunland Boulevard. Whipping a left on Sunland, he double-clutched, down-shifted, and gunned the Apache into the parking lot of Carter's Place. Licking his lips, he strode across the blacktop toward the bar. A couple of beers were definitely in order.

The tavern was noisy, loud with the voices of the hard-drinking regulars sitting at the tables and strung out along the bar. Sawdust covered the floor, and the jukebox blared a contemporary country ballad. The bartender waved to him as Philo made his way down the line of stools to his customary place at the end of the bar. He heaved himself onto the stool, signalling for a large draft.

The afternoon beer stop was a ritual for Philo, giving him a chance to uncoil before heading home. He downed the beer in three or four hefty gulps and pushed it out for a refill. Two stools away, the raucous voice of a fat, red-faced man could be heard above the din. The fat man was regaling his companion with dirty jokes and laughing uproariously. The guy was obnoxious, thought Philo, trying to ignore the fat man.

Philo reached into a bowl of peanuts sitting on the bar. He cracked them idly, popping the nuts into his mouth and dropping the shells on the floor. Another beer. Philo savored the golden liquid. Then, downing it, Philo laid a dollar bill on the bar and stood up. He reached into the peanut bowl, grabbed a handful, stuffed them into his pocket, and started for the door.

"Just a minit," said the fat man, swinging around on his bar stool to block Philo's way. "Why'nt ya just put 'em back." The fat man leaned forward on the stool, bringing his face close to Philo's belligerently.

"How's that?" said Philo, looking directly into the fat man's eyes.

The fat man leaned back, resting his elbows on the bar, still blocking Philo with his feet.

"You heard me," he said. "This ain't the Salvation Army. Put 'em back."

Philo looked at the fat man, his eyes crinkling. He reached into his pocket and withdrew several peanuts. "You mean these." It was more of a statement than a question. Philo's tone was flat. Had the fat man been more aware, he would have dropped the whole matter, but it was lost on him. He poked his companion in the ribs, inviting him to share in Philo's discomfort.

"Yeh asshole, 'nless you're takin' 'em to your tree." He laughed uproariously, poking his companion again. He took a sip of beer, coughing and sputtering at his own wit. "This squirrel," he said, choking with mirth, "is taking peanuts to his tree."

The fat man's companion, used to laughing at his jokes, tore himself away from a conversation with the bartender and turned to see what was going on. "What . . . what's that?" he said.

The fat man, staring, reached out and grabbed Philo's cheek between a thumb and forefinger.

"This squirrel," he said again, "is rippin' off peanuts." He squeezed Philo's cheek. "Ain't cha, squirrel?"

The fat man's friend spun around on the stool, a grin on his face. He took one look and the grin disappeared. His mouth dropped open and his eyes rolled to the top of his head. He tried to stop the fat man. There was no stopping him. Picking up his beer, the friend moved quickly to the far end of the bar. The fat man didn't notice, he was having too much fun. He guffawed.

"Gonna . . . carry . . . them . . . nuts . . . into . . . his . . . tree." He squeezed Philo's cheek harder. Philo stared at the man.

Imperceptibly Philo's hand closed around the peanuts. The fat man was so engrossed in his baiting he was unaware that everyone in the immediate vicinity had moved well out of the way. The jukebox continued to moan its tale of unrequited love.

The movement was too quick to be seen. One moment the fat man sat chuckling, grasping Philo's cheek. The next, his nose was mashed against his face. Peanuts and shells exploded from between Philo's knuckles to mix with the wet red mushroom that suddenly appeared just below the fat man's eyes. The fat man let out a bellow and charged off the bar stool fists flailing.

Philo stepped back, neatly catching the fat man with a jab to the head as he stumbled past. The fat man roared again as Philo's fists pounded into his gut. The fat man lunged. Philo wasn't there. He lunged again, trying to catch Philo. Philo sidestepped and chopped him neatly in the kidneys. The fat man grunted, careening into the bar. Instinctively he reached for something his hand closed around the handle of a metal lunch box. Swinging around, he brought it crashing down on Philo's head. The box flew open, sending half a sandwich and a Thermos bottle flying across the room. A red streak appeared on Philo's forehead where the lunch box cut him. Philo shook his head to clear the blood from his eye. He shouldn'ta done that, thought Philo.

Four triphammer blows to the midsection doubled the fat man over. A quick knee to the chin straightened him up again. The fat man bounced off the bar into a rain of blows to the head and gut. He was starting to sag. The fat man swung a roundhouse right. Philo ducked. The momentum of the blow carried the fat man around to meet an uppercut Philo brought up from the floor. It lifted the fat man off his heels, snapping his head back with a crack heard across the room. The fat man slid to the floor, his head lolling against the jukebox.

Philo hauled the man to his feet, almost tenderly, lifting him onto the bar stool.

The fat man's arms hung loosely at his sides, eyes uncomprehending, swollen shut, nose broken across his cheek. He stared vacantly as Philo spun him around. The music from the juke blared. Philo cocked his fist, then dropped his hand. It didn't matter. The fat man slid slowly off the stool and dropped into a pile on the floor. Cracking a peanut, Philo flipped the shell onto the fat man's belly, then turned and walked out of the tavern.

Crossing the parking lot to the Apache, Philo gingerly rubbed the cut on his forehead. He started the truck.

"California Countree" blasted out of the speakers. Philo grinned to himself, feeling the tingle in his knuckles and the warm sensation that always seemed to follow a fight or a piece of ass. He was still smiling as he moved out onto Sunland Boulevard.

Philo headed up the canyon, then down a dirt road past fruit trees, stucco houses, corrals, and horses. Driving easily now, the Apache churned up clouds of dust behind him. Philo popped another stick of gum into his mouth and laughed out loud. It was sure as hell good to be alive. Eucalyptus and scrub oak bordered the sides of the road. Ahead and to the left loomed a half acre littered with the remains of cars in various stages of death and disrepair. With a crank of the wheel, Philo turned into the driveway leading to a small frame-and-stucco house. Behind it sat another structure half the size. Philo's home.

Philo cranked the wheel again, narrowly missing Orville's ancient tow truck heading out of the driveway. Ma Boggs, Philo's feisty eighty-year-old landlady, sat next to Orville, bitching at her son's driving.

Orville, a lanky, grizzled man in his mid-thirties, stuck his head out of the two-truck window. He yelled as Philo rolled by, "Didja get the linkage?"

Philo nodded and waved as the tow truck creened across the unkept lawn and down across the curb into the street.

Philo continued up the driveway, braking in front of the small shed that sat next to his house. A camper shell rested against the shed. The temperature on the antique thermometer attached to the house's door frame read ninety-two degrees.

Orville Boggs contemplated his mother as they sped down the road, the tow truck bouncing catastrophically from side to side. He wondered what in hell he was doing. For the umpteenth time he was chauffeuring his mother to the Department of Motor Vehicles for another try at a licence. She'd failed the test so many times already he'd lost count.

"We're about there, Ma," he smiled at the old lady. "Maybe this time we'll get lucky."

"Luck hell!" replied Ma. "One way or t'other them sonsabitches is going to give me a licence."

"You'll make it," said Orville encouragingly. "We been through this so many times you're bound to pass sometime."

He deftly maneuvered the rig into the parking lot of the Department of Motor Vehicles, handily missing a fire hydrant and rolling to a screeching stop between a new Mercedes and a Cadillac. The man sitting in the Mercedes winced as the tow truck missed his rear end by half an inch.

Ma adjusted the rear-view mirror to get a look at herself. "I shoulda remembered my wig," she said, patting the sides of her wispy grey hair. "D'ya think it'll make any difference?"

"I don't know, Ma," said Orville. He scrunched down in the seat with an air of resignation. "I don't 'spect that's all they'll be lookin' at."

The old lady having finished her primping, fumbled in her handbag. Triumphantly, she withdrew a driver's manual and three long narrow sheets of paper, tests she had taken and failed before. Holding one of the sheets a half an inch from her eyes, she began mumbling the questions and answers to herself.

Orville, unslinging himself from the steering wheel, quickly stepped down from the cab of the tow truck. He made his way around the vehicle and opened the door on his mother's side.

"Don't be in such an all-fired big hurry," she grumbled. "I want to look at these here pictures one more time." She peered at the driver's manual intently. "I always did have trouble with these ones with the squiggly lines."

Orville rattled the door impatiently. "I hope you pass it this time," he said. "We're runnin' outta branches of this place to go to. They all know you."

"They don't know how I drive," said Ma. She stepped creakily down to the pavement. "Don't none of them know

13

how good I drive." She took Orville's arm as he slammed the cab door.

Making her way slowly toward the plate-glass doors of the DMV office, Ma Boggs shook her head. She shook her head again as they disappeared into the interior of the building. "I been driving before all a them sonsabitches was born."

Philo examined himself in the mirror above the sink in his Spartan digs. The cut on his forehead looked angry. Gingerly he wiped the congealed blood on a wet paper towel. Dumb sonofabitch oughtn't to have done that, he thought.

Philo walked to the refrigerator and opened a beer. He flicked on the radio. The familiar voice of the country boss jock faded into the opening strains of a new Charlie Rich hit. Philo hummed tunelessly, and checked the cut once again before making his way out the door.

He crossed the highway and headed toward the shed, cracking peanuts and discarding shells as he walked. Reaching the shed, Philo stuffed the remaining peanuts into his pocket and opened the door.

It was dark in the shed. Philo squinted, adjusting his eyes to the dim light. Cracks between the boards pencilled the specks of dust that danced in the sunlight. He looked to the right and left. The shed, as far as he could tell, appeared empty. He squinted again in the gloom.

Suddenly, 150 pounds of orangutan dropped on him from the rafters!

"Shit," grunted Philo, picking himself off the dirt floor. "I shoulda known." He turned and landed a glancing blow to the ape's head, receiving in return a backhand to the solar plexus, which doubled him over. Laughing for breath, Philo charged, catching the huge simian off balance. He hammered at the ape's body while the animal flailed at him with a hairy fist, holding onto Philo with one hand and pummelling him with the other.

Breaking free, Philo let loose a round-house, sending the

14

animal halfway across the shed. He followed with a left and a right, which the orangutan shrugged off with a grunt.

"Had enough?" asked Philo.

In answer, the ape bounded off the wall and leaped for a rafter beam. He swung back and forth for a moment, and then, with a mighty kick, knocked Philo ass over elbows out the door of the shed. Gibbering happily, he swung to the ground, his long arms outstretched, his teeth bared in a wide smile.

Philo grinned and scratched the ape's head. Reaching into his pocket, he withrew the peanuts and offered them. The ape, visibly brightening, took them from Philo's outstretched hand. Methodically he cracked one and placed it carefully into his mouth, smacking his lips with pleasure. He looked at Philo adoringly.

Philo rubbed his neck where the 150 pounds of hairy beast first descended on him. He took a peanut from Clyde's outstretched hand, hunkered down, and threw an arm affectionately around the beast's shoulders. Philo smiled. "You're getting mighty tricky, Clyde."

The glass door of the DMV swung open. Ma Boggs, her toothless jaw set in anger, marched defiantly from the building, followed by Orville.

"Don't feel bad, Ma," Orville said placatingly. "You passed the test. Didn't miss a one." He caught up with his mother.

"Yeah," she said. "I foxed 'em this time. They gave me the same test as I had right here." She thumbed through the stack of papers in her hand. "The one that starts with the bicycle question."

"You done real good, Ma." Orville's voice radiated reassurance, trying to snatch some victory from the jaws of defeat. Ma Boggs, however, was having none of it.

"Shithead waited till I passed this time b'fore tellin' me I was too old." She stomped her way to the truck and threw open the door.

"Shoulda remembered my wig," grumbled the old lady. She crawled into the cab and slammed the door. "Goddamn shitheads!"

Orville sighed. He wondered how many more times he was going to have to go through this before Ma got it into her head that the state was in no way going to issue her a licence.

By the time they arrived home it was dusk. "Next time," Ma said, "we gotta get outta town. Next time we're going up to Oxnard. None a them bastards know me there."

"Sure, Ma," said Orville glumly, "next time." He escorted her into the house.

It was dark when Orville exited the back door munching a banana and carrying a bag full of cherries. Philo was working under the '57 Chevy parked next to the shed.

The only thing still working on the car was the radio, which was blasting a guitar solo loud enough to be heard halfway to City Hall. A trouble light glowed from beneath the vehicle. Bugs flitted everywhere.

"Hey, Philo," Orville called out, his mouth full of banana. No response, just the pounding of a hammer on metal and the raucous twanging of the amplified guitar. "Hey, Philo!" Orville yelled, this time to make himself heard above the din. "You out there?"

Philo answered laconically from beneath the battered Chevy. "Naw, I ain't."

"Whatcha doin'?"

Philo scooted out from under the car and pointed to a chunk of twelve-by-twelve at Orville's feet. "Orville, you just asked me two dumb questions in a row. Bring me that block over there."

Orville set down the sack of cherries and picked up the block of wood. He carried it to the rear of the car, which was resting with a six-inch block under the axle.

"Ready?" asked Philo.

"Yeah . . . Okay!"

Philo stooped down, grabbing the rear bumper. He grunted, strained mightily, then heaved the rear end of the car eighteen inches off the ground. Orville, taking his time while Philo puffed and wheezed, kicked out the six-inch block and replaced it with the twelve-by-twelve. Philo set the car down with a thunk, looked at Orville, started to say something, then knowing it useless, changed his mind. Orville retrieved his cherries. Popping several into his mouth, Orville machine-gunned the pits at the side of the Chevy. They pinged satisfactorily against the metal.

"Ma's really pissed," said Orville between staccato bursts of pits. Philo looked up quizzically.

"It's Clyde. He got out this morning and came over. He shit all over everything."

"How'd she get him to go back?" Philo bent down to look under the car, hooking the trouble light onto a leaf spring.

"I think that's why she's so pissed. She had to bribe him with all of her Oreos."

"Well," said Philo, crawling under the car, "I'll make it up to her." Only his feet were visible as the hammering recommenced.

Orville munched reflectively on the cherries. "You got one goin' tomorrow, Philo?" he asked.

"Yeah." The voice from under the car was muffled. "You comin'?"

Orville grinned, upending the sack into his mouth. He wiped his chin with the back of his hand. "Sure am." He chuckled. "Yeah, I sure am."

TWO

The construction site was cleared and graded. Piles of lumber and stacks of steel and masonry were scattered around the area. A large sign standing at the corner of the lot depicted the architect's rendering of the completed project, a far cry from the current disarray. The pipe truck moved carefully into the site, threading its way through the mountains of building materials. It rolled to a stop behind a semitrailer. Philo leaned out of the cab, catching the attention of the semi's driver, who had just slammed and locked the big rear doors. He shouted above the noise of the engine and the blare of the portable radio.

"Where do they want this stuff?"

"Over there," yelled the driver. He indicated a spot across the yard, then climbed into his cab and cranked the diesel.

Philo waved acknowledgment. Shifting into reverse, he began backing toward the space. He moved the loaded rig smoothly, checking his clearances in the side mirrors. A ditch bordered one side of the unloading area. Philo gauged his distances. Cutting his wheels sharply, he double-clutched and split-shifted down. Philo was almost there when the noisy blast of a horn jolted him. Behind him, a loaded lumber truck, wheels churning, shot toward the empty space. Instinctively Philo spun the wheel to avoid him. The pipe truck bounced across several beams, the steering wheel spinning outrageously in Philo's hands. He jammed on the brakes and felt the wheels lock as the lumber truck sped past, squealing into the empty space. Philo's rig jolted sickeningly as the load shifted. Philo rammed the pedal. The truck swayed and lurched. Philo gunned the accelerator again. The truck bucked, shifted, and miraculously the load settled. Philo cut the ignition. His rear wheels rested half in, half out of the ditch. He gripped the wheel, jaw set. Philo was sweating. He could taste the saltiness.

The driver of the lumber truck poked his head out of the window. He yelled across the space that separated him from Philo. "Serves you right, you dumb sonofabitch. If you'd open your goddamn eyes . . ."

Philo uncoiled himself from the wheel. His knuckles were white. He punched open the door of the cab and slid to the ground, his face a mask. He headed toward the lumber truck as the driver jumped down from his cab. He moved toward Philo.

The semi had pulled to a halt, engine running. The driver held his breath as the two men approached each other. He could see the driver of the lumber truck moving angrily toward Philo. Then the lumber driver paused in mid-stride as the wave of recognition hit him.

His face changed expressions and hues like a kaleidoscope. He stumbled over himself, then backed away. Turning, he half ran, half slid, back to his truck. He jumped in, cranking the engine to life.

"Oh hey, man," he said. "I made a mistake. This is really your spot."

Philo paused, his eyes never leaving the driver's face.

"I didn't mean all that stuff," the lumber driver continued, mopping at his forehead. "Had a bad morning at the yard . . . Okay? . . . Sorry." He shifted the truck into gear and rapidly drove off to a far corner of the site.

Stoically, Philo watched him leave, then turned back to

his truck. The driver of the semi, pulling out of the site, waved as he rolled past. Philo grinned.

The driver turned and called out to his partner lying in the sleeper. "How much you putting down?"

A sleepy voice answered from the depths behind him. "A hunnert."

"You givin' or gettin'? yelled the driver.

"Gettin'," the sleepy voice answered.

"You're kiddin'," the driver shook his head unbelievingly. "You bettin' against him?"

"Eight to five," said the muffled voice, "Why?"

"We just passed Philo Beddoe."

The dishevelled head popped out of the sleeper.

"Yeah?" The voice was uncomfortable.

The driver grinned. "He was smiling."

The carrot and alfalfa fields flashed by, golden in the late-afternoon sun, as the Apache sped north toward Newhall. The ever-present country sounds still blared unrelentingly from the speakers. Philo, tapping his fingers rhythmically with the beat against the steering wheel, turned to Orville. Philo pointed to the glove compartment. "How about some gum," he said.

Orville, mesmerized by the heat and passing panorama, jerked himself away from the window and reached dutifully into the glove compartment. He broke open a new pack of gum, removed two sticks, and handed one to Philo. Wrappers disappeared out the window. Ahead, several semis stood grouped by the side of a small roadside cafe. A sign proclaimed the premises to be SYBIL'S and promised GOOD FOOD in foot-high letters. The semis parked around the aging building attested to the truth of the statement.

Philo eased the Apache off the blacktop and into the hard-packed dirt parking lot. He pulled up next to a semi just cranking up.

"Hey, Philo." The driver stuck his head out of the cab.

Philo acknowledged the greeting with a "Yeah, Marv" and a grin.

"How ya feeling today, Philo?" Marv's tone of voice seemed genuinely concerned.

"Don't worry, Marv. Everything's gonna be all right." Orville grinned.

"Eeehoo." Marv punched a button, letting out a blast on the air horns. "Honolulu, here I come." He laughed delightedly, revving the engine. Philo waved as the semi moved onto the highway with another blast of its air horns.

Making their way across the parking lot, Philo and Orville walked into the small cafe. Orville tripping across the threshold. Philo shook his head as Orville grinned sheepishly. He headed for the jukebox as Philo sat down at the counter. A couple of men sitting in a booth called out to him. Philo returned their greeting with a nod. Orville reached the jukebox and perfunctorily fed the machine several quarters.

"How's goin', Sybil?" asked Philo, reaching for one of the steaming mugs of coffee that the owner of the cafe set upon the counter.

"Same ol' horseshit," she said. "How's yerself?" She set the second cup on the counter next to Philo, waiting for Orville to finish punching buttons.

"Just fine," said Philo, "just fine."

Sybil wiped a hand across her forehead, pausing to tuck a few wisps of hair back into place. She could have cracked forty anytime in the past ten years, thought Philo affectionately. She'd been pushing coffee for so long her thumbs canted permanently at forty-five degrees. He took a sip of coffee as Sybil pulled a greasy spiral notebook from under the counter. She thumbed through the pages.

"Well, let's see what we got." She folded the pages over and peered at the almost illegible chicken scratches. "Just six this time, Philo. Total a three hundred. You're makin' 'em believers." She closed the notebook.

Reaching for his wallet, Philo removed five one-hundred-dollar bills. The jukebox jumped to life, Orville's favourites. More bars and cheating women. Orville plopped himself down beside Philo and reached for his coffee.

"You got twenty, Sybil?" asked Philo, pushing the hundreds toward her.

"Think I do," she said. She reached into the cash register and removed a bill, handing it to him. "Pretty soon you're gonna have to lay two to one 'stead a eight to five to get any action."

"Don't matter," said Philo.

Sybil chuckled. "You want to eat now or later?"

"What's the special?" Philo asked.

"Meat loaf."

He grimaced. "Later," he said, picking up his coffee and taking a large gulp. The hot liquid slid down his throat. His eyes searched Sybil's face. "Who?" he asked.

Sybil smoothed her hair back again and pointed with her head toward the back booth. "Him," she said. "Church."

Philo's eyes swung to the two men sitting at the rear of the cafe. There was no doubt whom she meant.

Both of them were uglier than sin, but the gorilla facing him looked like he could have tucked two of the other under his arms and still have had room for a couple more. He was barrel-chested with a thick neck that sloped to his shoulders in an unbroken curve, making his head seem smaller than it was. He was built big, but soft. The man's hands were like two huge hams resting on the table. Philo had seen enough.

The big man looked over at Philo. The big man stared, then turned abruptly to whisper to his companion. They appraised Philo carefully.

Philo took another swig of coffee. He caught Sybil's eye. "Church, huh . . ." He smiled. "Hail Mary!" He winked.

The conveyors of the cement factory stood stark and white against the sky, dwarfing the cars and trucks parked in the yard below. Tractor against trailer, the semis formed a large circle. Within the circle at least a hundred men congregated. The air was heavy and thick, with little hint of breeze.

Church stood in the centre of the circle. He had removed his checkered shirt and was swinging his hamlike hands. Limbering up. He grunted and took several deep breaths, allowing the air to escape slowly from his lungs. His companion kneaded the muscles of his thick neck and shoulders, mumbling words of encouragement.

Across the circle Philo stood with Orville, watching the huge man getting ready.

"He's pretty big," said Orville. "A mean-lookin' mother."

Philo nodded, removing his denim work shirt and handing it to Orville. Philo swung his arms in a wide arc, feeling the muscles taut beneath the skin. He was solid, not an ounce of excess fat, just sinew and muscle. Philo saw Church appraising him. Church was confident, sure that the difference in size and weight was in his favour. Church outweighed him by a good twenty pounds, was taller, and judging from the length of his arms probably had Philo on reach too. Philo noted Church's hands again. He'd have to watch those clubs.

The man who had been sitting with Church in the booth at Sybil's strode to the centre of the clearing. He looked around and cleared his throat. "Anybody here want to make a little side bet?" he asked. "Same odds." He looked from face to face. No one answered. "Got another hundred here . . . Don't tell me nobody wants it." He waited. Still no takers. "C'mon, now. He may be good, but he ain't no Tank Murdoch."

"Take it," Philo turned to Orville and motioned with his head.

"But that's all we got till . . ." Orville hesitantly reached into his pocket.

"Take it," said Philo again.

Orville sighed and called out to the man. "You're on." Holding the bills in his hand, he walked into the circle.

"Who's gonna hold it?" asked Church's companion.

"You hold it," said Philo.

The man took the money from Orville and backed off as Philo and Church moved toward each other. Voices from the crowd of truckers shouted encouragement.

The big man moved in. He lunged at Philo, aiming a roundhouse right at Philo's jaw. Had it connected, it would have torn his head off. Philo stepped back as Church lunged again. The right chopped at him, whistling past his ear. As Church passed, Philo jabbed with a left, snapping the heavier man's head back. With a roar, Church swung wildly. Philo ducked, sending a right to the midsection, doubling Church over. The big man fell back, catching his breath. Then he aimed a kick at Philo's groin. Sidestepping, Philo kicked Church's leg out from under him. He fell to the ground, landing heavily on his side with a loud grunt. Again, Philo stepped back as Church scrambled to his feet, pig eyes burning with hate. Church charged from a squat to meet a fistful of knuckles. He spat out a tooth and charged again, catching two quick ones to the jaw and gut. Stumbling, Church collapsed against the wheel of a truck.

Shaking his head to clear it, Church reached down and grabbed a handful of sand. Turning swiftly, he threw the sand into Philo's face, launching himself from the wheel. Church threw a punch that Philo deflected off his forearm, then walked into a right uppercut that should have floored a mule. He stood stunned not seeing the left that slammed into his gut, knocking the wind out of him. Two fast rights to the face and a left set him up. Philo launched an uppercut. It caught Church squarely on, the jaw, dropping him into the dirt. It was all over. Church was out on his face.

The truckers cheered, pounding each other on the back. All except those who had bet against Philo. Orville stepped up to Church's man. He was shaking his head in disbelief. His mouth hung open. Orville pulled the money from the man's hand and stuffed it carelessly into his pocket.

"Beer's on us," yelled Orville.

The truckers cheered again as they headed for their cabs. Back to Sybil's for some cold ones.

Philo contemplated Church lying mute in the dust. "Shit," Philo said to no one in particular. "He couldn't lick Clyde."

THREE

The Palomino Supper Club was jammed. New-talent Night for the hottest country-western club in the valley meant a shorter cover and cheaper booze than when a headliner was packing them in. The bullshit artists were out in force along with drinkers, diners, guitar pickers, and pickups.

A local bluegrass group stepped down from the bandstand to applause and melted into the crowd as the jukebox blared into life. Blessed relief for ears that had heard a whole lot less for the past hour. The smoke was thick enough to slice, hanging like smog over the cluttered bandstand.

Philo and Orville were at the bar taking it all in, bottles in hand, a couple of empties sitting beside them. Opposite, at a table, a couple of dollies were animatedly eating and talking.

Philo sipped his beer and eyed the girl nearest him. Not too bad, he thought, turning around to get a better look. The girl was wolfing down a bowl of chowder, conversing with her friend between spoonfuls. She looked up for a second, catching Philo's stare, then busied herself again with her chowder. Philo continued staring. The girl's friend excused herself and stumbled off toward the restroom.

Philo swung himself off the stool and moved to the table.

He slid in across from the girl. "How do," he said. "My name's Philo."

The girl continued spooning chowder into her mouth.

"You don't mind if I sit here and rest a spell, now, do ya?" Philo settled back against the vinyl, giving her a grin.

The girl looked up from the bowl, appraised him narrowly, then spooned another mouthful. "Suit yourself," she said, not missing a beat.

"I don't remember seein' you here before," Philo said. He tapped his fingers on the table uncomfortably and took a swig from the bottle.

"I've never been here before." She took another mouthful, her eyes never leaving the bowl.

Philo squirmed in his seat, beginning to wish he had stayed at the bar. "What do you do when you're not here?" The question didn't sound quite right, and the girl was giving him no help at all.

She laid down her spoon. "My name is Carol. I go to USC. I major in sociology and I'm here because I'm doing a paper on the country-western mentality."

Philo smiled. Whatever this bitch's trip was, it definitely didn't include him. "You just blew two minutes of our conversation," he said, still trying to salvage something.

"You asked if you could sit," she countered. "Didn't say nothin' about talking."

"Whoeee," said Philo. "Who you mad at?"

The girl pointedly ignored the question and fumbled in her purse till she found her cigarettes. Pulling one out, she stuck it into her face. "Have you got a match?" she asked. Her tone was definitely not conducive to romance.

"Nope," said Philo. "Don't smoke." He took another pull at his beer.

The girl looked heavenward, disgust plainly written on her face. She scooted out of her chair and walked to the bar. Cheerist! thought Philo. He caught Orville's eye and motioned to him.

Orville slid off the stool and ambled over to the table.

"How you makin' out?" He jerked a thumb at the girl.

Philo smiled, holding out his hand. He winked. "Hand 'em over," he said.

For a moment Orville stood uncomprehending. Then he let out a chortle. They'd done this before. Opening his mouth, Orville pulled out twenty-one hundred dollars' worth of false teeth and deposited them wetly into Philo's hand. Philo plopped them into the girl's chowder and sat back, a beatific grin on his face. Orville, staying close to the action, took a swallow of beer and damn near choked on it.

"What," said Philo, as Carol returned, cigarette aflame, "is the country-western mentality?"

She sat back and puffed several times, regarding him through half-closed eyes, weighing her response. She smiled. "Well, if the lyrics of the songs are any indication, it's somewhere between moron and dull normal." Triumphantly she stubbed out the cigarette and attacked her chowder.

"How do," said Orville, grinning at Carol's girlfriend, who had threaded her way back from the restroom. His mouth was a cavernous hole. "My name's Orville." The girlfriend looked at him, wincing with distaste.

The MC climbed onto the bandstand just as Carol dipped her spoon into the chowder. She raised it to her lips. Hanging from the spoon and smiling at her in a half-familiar fashion were the dripping set of dentures. Her eyes grew round. For a moment she was speechless, her mouth opening and closing spasmodically, then she let out a shriek. The teeth plopped back into the bowl as the spoon clattered to the table.

Philo reached nonchalantly across the table and picked the dentures out of the bowl. "Well, I'll be goddamned!" He handed the dripping teeth to Orville, who popped them back into his maw. "'N all the time I thought it was a man's balls you was after." He smiled at Carol. Orville licked the remains of chowder from his lips.

Looking at Philo in disbelief and horror, Carol grabbed

her purse and ran from the room, closely followed by her girlfriend as applause for the singer the emcee introduced filled the room. "So here she is, first time at the Palomino . . . Lynne Halsey-Taylor."

The voices in the room hushed as the girl on the stage started to sing. A soft country ballad that took Philo back to gentler times. She was beautiful. No, not that really, but fresh and young, with something indefinable that reached out and grabbed Philo with a soft urgency he had never experienced before. He watched her face, only half hearing the words of the song. For a moment their eyes met, and then it was gone and the girl moved into the chorus.

Philo took a deep breath, got up from the table, and returned to the bar. Orville followed, still convulsed.

"Did you see her face?" Orville slapped his thigh. "You coulda' put a turd in there'n she couldn'ta got a better look on her . . . ."

"Hold on t' yerself, Orville," shushed Philo. "I want to hear this." He nodded in time to the music, losing himself in the song and the girl.

The song closed to mild applause, but Philo was ecstatic. He was still clapping as the crowd turned back to their conversations and beer. The girl hopped off the bandstand, guitar in hand, and headed in his direction.

"Orville," said Philo, "I can tell you're gettin' awfully bored sittin' here at the bar."

"Huh?" said Orville, setting down his beer.

Philo motioned with his head toward the approaching girl. "Wouldn't you like to get some air?"

Orville followed Philo's gaze. "Oh," he said. "Oh yeah, sure, Philo." He nodded good luck and moved off to find his own.

The girl lay the guitar on the bar and glanced up. She smiled. Philo grinned back. She motioned to the bartender. "Excuse me," she said, "but could I leave my guitar back here for a time?"

34

"Sure can," said the bartender. He slid the guitar off the bar and stashed it behind him.

"You sure did sing pretty," said Philo.

The girl looked at him, brushing the hair back from her face. "Thank you," she said. She waited, smiling at him.

"I'd be happy if you let me buy you a drink," said Philo. He leaned back on the bar, feeling the excitement of her standing next to him.

"I'd like a beer," she said.

Philo held up two fingers for the bartender. He nodded and set them in front of Philo.

"I missed your name when the emcee introduced you." He handed the girl a beer. "Mine is Philo Beddoe."

She took the beer from his hand. Philo felt a momentary shock as their fingers touched.

"Lynne Halsey-Taylor," she grinned. "You have a fight with your girlfriend?"

"Huh . . .? Oh you mean that." Philo smiled and shook his head.

"She ran mighty quick."

"Well, I hardly knew her a minute."

Lynne ran a finger over the perspiring surface of the cold bottle. "You sure must go through a lot of women."

They both laughed. Philo took a swallow, wiping his mouth with the back of his hand. He looked at her, feeling a warm glow spread through his body. "That sure was a fine song you were singing. You write that?"

Lynne drank from her bottle and shook her head. "Wish I did. That's an old Edy Lynne tune. My daddy used to sing it to me when I was little."

"Maybe that's where I know you from," said Philo.

Lynne looked at him, a question on her face.

Philo continued. "When you was little . . . I was in love with a little girl in the third grade. Looked enough like you to make my memory water."

"You know," she said, smiling, "you talk funny."

Philo smiled back at her. They sat looking at each other

as the emcee introduced another act, a pimply-faced youth who sang of love and betrayal.

Philo shook his head. "It's gettin' awfully smoky in here. I don't suppose you'd . . . ."

Lynne answered his unfinished question, "I'd love to."

The Apache cruised across the San Fernando Valley, Lynne singing softly to the country ballad playing on the radio. The valley at this time of night was almost romantic. The Santa Ana winds had blown away the smog, and the stars overhead outlined the dark backdrop of the San Gabriels. The smell of sage wafted through the cab. Fields of early corn shimmered in the moonlight. Lynne rested her head against Philo's shoulder.

Since leaving the Palomino, they talked and laughed with a free and easy naturalness that surprised Philo. It was as if he had known the girl all his life. Her warmth and interest broke down his initial reticence to talk, and he found himself opening to her like he'd never done before. Discovering each other was exhilarating. Philo pressed her to tell him about herself. He wanted to know everything and he didn't want it to end.

"And so I decided that there was nothin' I liked better'n singin', and so here I am." She snuggled against his arm.

"Sure am glad," Philo said, caressing her shoulder.

"That I like singing?" She looked up at him.

Philo smiled and pulled her closer. "That here y'are."

The truck approached a trailer park. Philo cramped the wheel, turning into the entrance.

"That's it," said Lynne. "Over there, the fifth one."

Philo pulled over to the side and cut the ignition.

"Row No. 3," she said. "That's my lucky number." She looked at him from half-closed eyes. Philo reached for her.

"You're *my* lucky number." Philo pulled her to him, feeling her melt. She turned her face up as he sought her lips. The kiss was deep and lingering. She pressed herself against him, her hand caressing the back of his neck. He came up for air reluctantly, then gently opened her lips. Her tongue invaded his mouth. The heat rose from him, rolling, cascading through his body. He shivered, feeling her respond to him. He kissed her again, then, breaking away, whispered urgently. "I don't suppose you'd like to ask me in for . . . uh, whatever?"

"I'd love to . . . only . . ." She hesitated.

Philo kissed her, pressing her to him. "Only . . .?"

Her tongue caressed his ear and she nibbled at his lobe. A rush. "Only my boyfriend, Schyler, is sleeping."

Philo jerked back. A bucket of ice water. His passion receded like a southbound freight. "Your . . . uh . . ."

Lynne moved against him, pulling him to her, her lips brushing his. "Oh, he wouldn't mind . . ." she whispered after a moment.

"He wouldn't?" Philo sat back, looking at her in confusion.

"Uh-uh. Just so long as you don't try to drive his car." She snuggled against him.

"If it's all the same to you . . ." Philo looked at her searchingly, surprised and more than a little perturbed, "uh . . . later?"

Lynne moved away from him, smoothing her hair. She searched his face carefully for a moment, then smiled. She touched his cheek with her hand, then wordlessly opened the door and walked slowly to the trailer. She hesitated for a second, then entered. The trailer door clicked shut.

Philo stared ahead, into the darkness.

FOUR

Morning. The valley, hot and dry, but cooler in the Apache with the windows open as Philo and Clyde sped down Roscoe. The ape bounced comfortably in the seat in time to the ever-present country music.

Philo had temporarily resolved the events of the night before, the girl, the boyfriend, the situation. All of that stuff had happened before he'd met her. Now, it would be different. It was all going to change. He would make it change. Philo smiled. He'd be seeing her again and that was all that really mattered. He sat back in the seat, his mind tranquil.

The Apache pulled up to an intersection for the light. The staccato roar of two chopped motorcycles jolted Philo out of his reverie. They pulled alongside. Philo regarded the bikers with indifference as they eyed the Apache. Both were long-haired and bare-armed. Levi-jacketed "clubbers," their Black Widow colours were crawled all over them. The tank of one hog bore the same insignia. Beneath the paint job of the second Harley, a vivid L.A.P.D. logo could be seen.

"Hey man, look at that," said one of them above the bark of the engines. "A fuckin' ape!" A German helmet sprouting two steer horns was jammed on the biker's head.

"Which one?" drawled the other, a tall, heavily muscled man wearing a filthy derby and eye patch.

Steer horns laughed, pointing a finger at Clyde, who was staring at him disdainfully. The laughter turned to a frown as Clyde casually smirked at him and rotated his index finger in the vicinity of his ear. The biker glared at him.

"What'd you say?" He turned to Eye Patch. "Hey, you see what he said?!"

"It ain't hard to understand," said Philo, leaning over Clyde to stare directly at the bikers. "He thinks you stink from dumb."

Clyde, obviously pleased by the interchange, gibbered and smacked his lips with glee, pounding the door of the Apache with his hairy fist. The derbied biker gunned his engine angrily, then arrogantly flicked his wet stogie directly into Clyde's face.

The ape screamed, grabbing at his eyes, grunting in pain. The light changed.

"So long, ape shit!" yelled Steer Horns, kicking his bike into gear. Both choppers squealed off down the street, their riders laughing upraoriously.

Furious, Philo peeled after them, his tires smoking on the hot pavement. The motorcycles were half a block ahead when they wheeled around, coming past Philo going the other way. Philo hit the brakes and cut the wheels hard, spinning out and damn near clipping an oncoming camper. Cramming the Apache into second, he skidded around a corner, narrowly missing a mailbox. He dumped it into third as he came up on the bikers' tails. His eyes were blazing.

Eye Patch turned, saw Philo on his ass, and gunned full throttle past Steer Horns, jerking his thumb back. Steer Horns looked back. His face fell. The wrath of God and his simian sidekick barrelled down on him. He hit the throttle and shot past his partner with a yell. Both bikes roared through the intersection on yellow. The light flashed as Philo sandwiched through, cutting his wheels sharply,

42

swerving around the front end of a Dodge van and shooting between two pedestrians. The bikes pulled ahead. Philo floored it again as the choppers cut down an alley. He down-shifted and slid around the corner on two wheels, catching a piece of stucco wall.

Ahead of him, the bikers were bouncing and slipping through the dirt. Philo gained on them. Eye Patch shook his fist as the bikes found blacktop, and screamed down the highway, the Apache in hot pursuit. An IN 'N' OUT BURGER loomed ahead. The bikes leaned precariously as they turned up the driveway and passed the speakers.

"Your order, please," rasped a tinny voice. The bikes dropped into second, throttled down, and wove their way around the line of cars waiting for greasy hamburgers and imitation milk shakes.

Philo ground the Apache into low and bounced over the curb, engine screaming. A car blocked his way.

"Your order, please," grated the speaker. Philo hit the brakes and shoved the Apache into reverse.

"Shit!" he yelled in frustration as the choppers moved through the IN 'N' OUT BURGER and disappeared up a side street.

The shocked girl at the mike looked at the boy packaging fries. It was gonna be a long day.

Philo swung onto the highway and rounded the corner at fifty. The bikers were specks in the distance. Flooring the Apache, he covered three blocks to their one. Philo smiled. The bikers, flanked by houses and blocked by a golf driving range, were headed into a dead end. Philo hit the accelerator, weaving across the road in case they had it in mind to come back through him. The bikers looked around. Philo was less than a block away, and coming fast. The two bikes roared through the parking lot, past highly polished, lowered chariots in a high-school low-riders' competition, around the Bucket o' Balls booth, and down onto the driving range. Screaming right behind them, Philo didn't hesitate. Clyde closed his eyes as Philo blasted through the high wire fence.

A dozen golfers paid no attention to the bikes, or the Apache ripping down the range. Balls pinged and bonked against the truck, bouncing off the windshield and the bed. The bikers rode screaming through a hailstorm of balls that bounced and ricocheted off helmet and head. Clyde, in a frenzy of excitement, jumped up and down, banging on the roof, twirling and burbling in rapture.

The choppers, Philo hot on them, screeched out of the rain of golf balls, through the fence, and back into the street, where they opened it up, finally putting some distance between them. Eye Patch grinned, flipping Philo the bird as he barrelled around the corner into an arterial.

Philo slid from the side street onto the highway in a four-wheel drift, moving down the arterial, off again, then down an alley adjacent to a car wash. The attendants looked up as the bikers catapulted past them. Cutting a hard left, Steer Horns charged into the churning maelstrom of the wash. Eye Patch followed. Brushes swirled and twirled. Water jetted and sprayed. The bikes rolled past a slow-moving Toyota as the Apache, wheels spinning, roared into the tunnel behind them. The Toyota blocked his way. Philo down-shifted, catching the smaller car just under the bumper with his front end. Accelerating, he shoved the little import before him. It caromed off both walls, bouncing between the brushes and white-wall steamers.

Steer Horns came out first, his helmet brightly polished, followed by Eye Patch, both washed, hot-waxed, and trailing clouds of soapy bubbles. The screeching and scraping of metal on metal issued from the depths of the wash. The Toyota burst from the exit like a shot from a cannon, slid sideways through the racks of drying towels, and rolled slowly to rest beside its ashen-faced owner.

The Apache charged out of the tunnel like a Tijuana bull on the prod. Philo gunned it past the screaming customers, as several employees dropped their rags, heading for home before the law arrived. Philo whipped back onto the highway, catching sight of the two Black Widows ahead of him. He punched it to the floor. The bikers turned off the highway, rode down a side street, then turned onto the frontage road that ran beside the railroad tracks.

Philo tore out of the side street, tromping it. He was only fifty yards behind. Both Widows looked over their shoulders. Eye Patch angrily flipped Philo the finger again. This guy was sticking to them like stink on shit.

A street sweeper, brushes churning and water spraying, moved out from behind a line of parked cars. The bikes were headed right for him. Both bikers swerved sharply, missing the sweep, but hitting the water, hydroplaning and fishtailing all over the road. Out of control, the bikes careened across the street and flew into a field of newly fertilized alfalfa, throwing their riders. The bikers, dazed, sat up and wiped the shit from their faces.

Philo grinned triumphantly and bore down upon the two. Clyde, in an ecstasy of excitement, climbing and jumping all over the cab, knocked the keys from the ignition. As the engine died, the two Widows took off running across the field. Grabbing the keys, Philo stuck them into the ignition. The engine cranked but wouldn't catch. Philo slammed the dashboard with his fist and jumped out of the truck. He ran to the street sweeper and jumped on, heaving the started driver from his seat. Slamming the sweeper into gear, Philo took off after the running bikers.

Seeing Philo at the controls of the sweep, Clyde piled out of the Apache and loped after the yellow monster. Catching hold, he swung onto the machine, settling himself with a grunt next to Philo.

A train whistle shrieked in the distance. The two bikers, seeing the yellow juggernaut descending upon them, turned and raced for the tracks. By this time both Black Widows were sure that Philo was crazy and it was entirely possible they might not survive if he caught up with them. Jumping, stumbling, and falling, they crossed a small irrigation ditch, jumped a barbed-wire fence, and ran alongside the tracks.

45

Philo followed. The sweeper was wide open, its engine screaming and protesting as it bounced across the irrigation ditch and tore through the barbed-wire fence. Eye Patch picked up several stones, cursing as he threw them at the yellow machine.

Churning sticks and rocks, and spraying water, brushes whirling, the sweeper bore down on the bikers. Looking down the tracks, they saw the freight approaching. They headed for it.

Philo cursed as the new direction the bikers took put distance between them. Jumping off the sweeper, he pounded after the two, narrowing the gap as the train grew closer. The sweeper, with Clyde now at the controls, rapidly churned toward a loading dock beside the tracks where several men were filling a freight car with crates of fruits and vegetables. Clyde hooted with joy as the machine headed up the ramp, then down the platform. The freight loaders looked up in disbelief. Then with cries of terror, they leaped off both sides of the platform as the sweeper came tearing through. Crates and boxes disintegrated, shredded greens filled the air. The behemoth sped on toward the end of the platform, leaving a wake of melon rind and squashed bananas. An eight-foot drop loomed ahead.

The moving freight train was now almost even with the dock.

The bikers launched themselves at the ladders of the freight cars, with Philo running a hair's breath behind them. On the platform the sweeper headed inexorably toward its doom, with Clyde pushing and pulling levers with happy abandon, blissfully unaware of impending disaster.

Steer Horns leaped, catching the ladder by one rung and holding on for dear life. His companion screamed for him to wait. The last freight car was rolling by. Philo was less than two feet away and bent on murder. The frantic Widow screamed and jumped for the tail end of the freight. A lucky grab; his fingers closed around a ladder rung just in time.

Philo leaped . . . and landed face first in the dirt. Getting to his feet, Philo turned to see the street sweeper cascading off the end of the concrete pier. A furry bundle leaped from the dying machine just as it toppled over the edge, nose-dived, crashed, and rolled over, expiring in a gush of water and steam. As Philo was wishing he could be there to hear the sweeper driver's explanation, 150 pounds of hair, muscle and love jumped off the loading dock, ran through the freight car and slammed into him, knocking him down. As the train receded into the distance, Philo rolled down the embankment next to the tracks, imprisoned in the iron embrace of a grinning and adoring Clyde.

Night. The valley cooler now, as the Apache rolled out Lankersheim, North Hollywood's main drag. KGBS "Gentle Country" drifted from the box. The stars were out, promising another smog-free day. Philo reached over and pulled Lynne to him. She smiled and touched his lips with her finger, singing softly to the song on the radio. Philo waited for her to finish. The song wound down and as Lynne hummed the closing bars, she looked up at him and saw the question in his eyes. She snuggled next to him, taking his hand and smoothing the fingers. Philo looked down at her, framing the question he was about to ask.

"Why you with him if you don't like him?"

She hesitated, caressing his hand. "He promised he'd help me to get the seven thousand dollars."

"For what?" He felt the tips of her fingers.

"The down payment." Lynne began singing again as the jock punched in the No. 5 song of the week. The melody was sad and sweet. Philo listened to her, waiting. The song ended.

"What do you want to buy?"

She leaned back in the seat and took a breath. "My own club, back home in Denver. So's I can sing anytime I want to. I'm gonna call it the Halsey-Taylor Drinking Fountain. That'll be the name of my group too. I'll have New-talent Night three times a week."

"How much you got of that seven thousand dollars?" He reached out and touched her neck.

"He won't tell me." She looked down at her hands.

"The only thing I got worth near any money," he said, shaking his head and smiling, "is Clyde."

"Clyde?"

"He's my ape. I won him in a fight."

"You won him?"

"Yeah. He was brought over for the zoo, to make a baby."

"You mean, like he's from Africa?"

"No," said Philo. "Sumatra, but when he got here, the other male orang had already got it done."

"I don't understand," said Lynne.

"Well, after that, Clyde got so mean, they sold him to a zoo in the desert."

"The desert?"

"You know them places. They say 'See the dragon! Cactus candy five miles.' Like that."

"And?"

"That's where I won him. I bet my truck and two dirt bikes."

"You must have wanted him a lot."

Philo shrugged. "I just couldn't stand seein' him in that cage."

"Who did you fight for him?" She took his hand again, interlacing their fingers.

"Four guys," said Philo. He grinned disparagingly.

"You'd think they'da give up after the first few lost."

"Oh no," he said, matter-of-factly. "I fought 'em all at once."

Lynne looked at him, her eyes questioning. "You like to fight."

"Used to like to . . . better'n anything." He then looked at her. "Well, almost anything."

She laughed. "How come you don't do it professional?"

"I don't like it like that," he said. "Too many people tellin' you what to do . . . This way it's been fun."

48

"You're a regular Tank Murdoch."

Philo turned to her, a note of interest in his voice. "Huh? . . . You know him?"

Lynne nodded. "Just about him. He lives in Denver. He's a regular institution."

Philo shook his head in agreement. "That's the one guy I'd like to meet," he said.

"Well," said Lynne, "the one guy I'd like to meet is Clyde."

"You gotta meet Orville first. He's waitin' for us." Philo smiled. She squeezed his hand.

Sybil's cafe was half full. Philo, Orville, and Lynne were finishing their meal.

"And so," Lynne said, "Tank Murdoch was in the back seat of this ol' car with this debutante. Her daddy owned most of the town. And Tank's buddy was in the trunk."

Orville, breathless with anticipation, urged her on. "What happened then?"

Two bikers, resplendent in the colours of the Black Widows, arrogantly strolled into the cafe. They eyed the crowd, then stalked to the counter, dropping heavily into the seats. They noticed Lynne.

"Well," said Lynne, "she was such a pure little thing . . . that nobody'd believe the stories that Tank was tellin'."

"Well," said Orville, repeating himself, " what happened then?"

Philo looked at Orville as Lynne continued demurely. "You just gotta use your imagination, Orville. But after, when she heard him bumpin' around and laughin' in the trunk, she started to scream." Lynne looked at Orville, who was listening in rapt attention, his mouth hanging open. She winked at Philo. "And that's when the cops came. Musta been six or eight of them. Tank tried to explain, but of course they all knew him and nobody was listenin'. Anyway, before it was over, he put four a them cops in the hospital and it took twelve more a them to take him in."

49

"Man!" said Orville. He shook his head in respect to the prowess of Tank Murdoch.

"Only one thing I wonder about in a story like that," said Philo.

"What's that?" asked Lynne.

"Who remembered to let that guy outta the trunk of the car?!"

The three of them laughed. "Shit," said Orville. "He's probably still in there." They laughed again.

The waitress, hovering nearby for a break in the conversation, set a beer in front of Lynne. The waitress was nervous and apologetic. "Those people at the counter over there," she pointed at the two bikers who were staring at Lynne with unconcealed lust, "they asked me to bring this to the lady. I'm really sorry." She hurried away.

Philo looked at the two bikers. Then, taking the beer from in front of Lynne, he took a large swig. He smiled at the bikers, nodding his head in thanks.

Elmo, the smaller of the two, looking more like an Encino hairdresser than a biker, glanced at his companion and got up from his seat. Swaggering to where Philo, Orville, and Lynne were sitting, he stuck his arm under Philo's nose. "You see that?" he asked.

Philo looked at the arm closely, touching it with one finger as though it were a dead fish. "An arm?" He looked at Elmo and smiled.

"That!" said Elmo, pointing at the tattoo of a spider.

Philo turned to Orville and gave him a questioning glance. Orville leaned over the table to peer seriously at the arm. He studied it, then sat back, nodding in agreement. He smiled at Elmo.

"A tattoo," said Philo emphatically.

Not used to this type of treatment and beginning to feel that he needed some support, Elmo motioned to Frank, who lurked behind him. He was big, muscular, wearing a headband and looking like Geronimo.

"They don't know what this is," said Elmo petulantly,

pointing at his spider.

Frank studied Philo and Orville carefully through half-closed eyes, then slowly and with deliberation thrust his sinewy arm in front of Orville. There was an identical spider tattooed on it.

Orville grabbed the arm and scrutinized it closely, bringing his nose to within a half an inch of the design. He sneezed, spraying the spider, quickly apologizing. Then, thrusting the arm away, he reached across the table to grab Elmo's arm. A look of amazement crossed his face as he leaned over and whispered in Philo's ear.

Philo nodded his head. Triumphantly he turned to the two bikers. "Two tattoos?"

"Them's black widdas," announced Elmo angrily.

Frank looked from Orville to Philo with a practiced stare. "More people," Frank said slowly, "die from black widows than rattlers every year." He stepped back an inch, waiting for the effect.

"Is that right?" said Orville. "Ya know, I appreciate knowing that. Most people I know jest step on 'em 'n' squish 'em."

Elmo's face took on a reddish hue, the veins pulsing in his neck. He balled his fist menacingly.

"Now, Orville," said Philo, "that's no way to talk to somebody who just bought us a brew. Why'n't you settle up here. I'm gonna step right outside with these boys and thank 'em properly." He looked at Elmo, the smile still on his face.

More than a flicker of apprehension crossed Elmo's eyes as Philo stood and loomed a foot above his head. Frank, now having second thoughts, pushed Elmo toward the door.

Philo got up from the table. He turned to Lynne. "Jest be a minute," he said. He followed the two bikers out the door of the cafe.

Lynne, a look of concern on her face, turned to Orville, who was taking the last bite of his pie. "Shouldn't you go 'n' . . ."

Orville stuffed the last morsel into his mouth and smiled.

"Sure is fine pee-can pie," he said. He dropped a couple of bills on the table and rose slowly. They made their way to the cash register. Orville paid the bill. Outside, subdued sounds of bone meeting flesh, grunts, groans, and then silence. Finally, Orville pushed open the door. They stepped outside.

Philo was standing with his back against the wall. Behind him in the trash bin, four pairs of boots protruded grotesquely. Several yards from the bin were two Harley choppers, chrome gorgeous. Both sported the Black Widow insignia on their tanks. Philo gazed at the choppers, a half smile on his lips.

"Orville," Philo nodded in the direction of the Apache, "pull the truck over to here."

Orville and Lynne climbed into the cab. Sticking it into reverse, Orvrville backed the Apache to where Philo was standing and stepped out of the cab. Philo released the tailgate, and then with a mighty heave lifted one of the bikes and set it into the bed of the truck. A moment later the second bike joined its companion. Laughing, they rolled down the highway, the Harleys in the bed bouncing crazily to a hot one from "California Countree."

FIVE

The disc grated and rasped on metal as Philo finished sanding the Black Widow decal off the bubble tank. The bike he was working on was in pieces, piled neatly beside the modified frame. Another bike, new orange popsicle paint gleaming, rested on two milk crates — complete except for wheels.

Clyde sat, brooding in the sun, contemplating a polka-dot housedress hanging on the line. He stared at it, fascinated as it flapped in the breeze. A full belly, the hot sun, the noise, and the flapping garment stirred strange half-forgotten jungle memories. He grunted and smacked his lips, methodically stripping a dead branch of its crackling leaves. He stuffed the leaves into his mouth, chewing reflectively.

Philo continued to sand, pulling the goggles back in place, touching the edge of the sander to the final spot of black paint on the bare stainless-steel tank. He felt a jab in the ribs. He shrugged it off, continuing with his work. He felt the jab again. "Knock it off, Clyde," he said. He rubbed the spot he was working on with his forefinger, then brought the disc to the metal surface once more. This time the cane whacked him across the back of his head. Angry, he spun around. Ripping off his goggles, he found himself face to face with Ma Boggs.

"Oh . . . Ma," said Philo, rubbing the back of his head where she'd cracked him. "Now, what did you go and do that for?"

"Been tryin' t' get yer attention fer five minutes," grumbled the old lady. She tapped the cane on the ground. "Did ya see Orville?"

"Yeah, I seen 'im." Philo continued to rub the back of his head.

"Well?" The old lady waited for an answer. Philo, not knowing quite what she wanted, remained silent.

"Orville tell ya what?" she continued.

Clyde, unable to resist, ambled over to the line and yanked the polka-dot dress.

"Oh yeah," said Philo, wrapping the cord around the sander. "I'm sorry you didn't get your licence again."

"That ain't the what, what I mean." Ma Boggs glared at Philo.

Philo nodded. He knew what she was leading up to. "Clyde . . . Sorry, Ma, he don't usually do things like that."

In the background Clyde leisurely dipped the polka-dot dress into a bucket of water and began to wash the Apache with it. The great streaks of grime he was producing pleased him immensely.

"Well," said Ma, "what are you gonna do about it?"

"The crap or the Oreos?"

"About Clyde, goddammit!" The old lady forcefully jabbed the tip of her cane into the ground. "I don't have no privacy in my own home no more."

"Well, I confronted him about it," said Philo. He laid the sander down. "I don't s'pect he'll do it again."

The sopping dress caught on the door handle of the truck and ripped. Clyde gazed at the half that remained in his hand. Puzzled, he tentatively touched the piece that remained sticking on the door. An enigma.

Ma Boggs continued beratingly. "Rented to one person cuz I want my privacy. Don't have no privacy no more."

"Clyde's gettin' awfully strong, Ma," said Philo placatingly. "But I got a new lock. He won't bother you no more."

"Hmmph," grumbled Ma. She turned and began walking slowly toward the back door of the house. "No privacy in yer own home no more . . . new lock . . . Hummph . . . a whole bran'-new bag of Oreos."

At the word "Oreos," Clyde's eyes lit up. As the old lady passed by, he tossed the rag into the air and reached out. A hairy hand snaked around her neck. Cradling the old lady's head in his palm like a coconut, he drew her to him. Pursing his simian lips, he wetly planted on hers the sweetest kiss this side of Sumatra.

"Aarrgh!" Ma Boggs jerked out of the creature's grasp and spat three times. "Goddammit . . . Stop that!" She pushed at the offending ape, who was reaching for her again. "Goddamn baboon . . . no respect . . . no privacy . . . no nothin' . . ." She spat again, wiping Clyde's wetness from her lips. "Shit!" Angrily she stomped her way to the house. Philo glared at Clyde.

"Okay, Clyde, I warned ya."

Clyde sheepishly peered from beneath his armpit. He squeaked questioningly, adoring and forlorn.

Philo pointed at him with a forefinger, his thumb cocked back like a hammer. "Bang!" he said.

Clyde, knowing he'd been shot, leapt high into the air, then collapsed into a pile at Philo's feet. He lay motionless, a limp cadaver, eyes closed. Then, unable to resist, a hairy hand lovingly grasped Philo's ankle.

The Palomino was jammed as usual. Lynne waved to Philo from the bandstand across the heads of the crowd. She finished her song, jumped down from the stage, and joined him. Sliding the guitar to the bartender, she grabbed Philo's arm. "Let's get outta here," she said.

Philo downed his beer and guided her out of the club, holding her close. Crossing the parking lot, he opened the door of the Apache and helped her in. She kissed him lightly. He climbed into the cab, started the engine, and pulled onto Lankersheim, flipping on the radio. Lynne snuggled next to him.

"They sure like you," he said after a moment, his own feelings apparent but unspoken.

She pressed his arm in thanks.

Reaching into his jacket pocket, Philo withdrew a thick manilla envelope and handed it to her.

"What's this?" asked Lynne. She took the envelope from his hand.

"Open it."

Lynne hefted the envelope, weighing it. "Sure feels heavy." She lifted the flap with a fingernail and looked inside. Forty fifty-dollar bills. Two thousand dollars. She ran her thumb over the edge of the green, amazed. "Philo! Where did you get it?!"

"Off a couple ol' widows." He kept his face straight in mock seriousness, noting her look of puzzlement.

She caught on and grinned. "You mean . . ."

Sitting back rigidly in the seat, Philo ponderously imitated Frank's serious voice. "More people wantin' t' buy widow bikes than die by rattler's bite every year."

"Oh Philo!" She hugged him; laughing, they drove into the night.

The days that followed passed quickly, blending together in a montage of feelings and events that left Philo dazed and happy. The hours he spent with Lynne had a vague, dreamlike quality, as though he were inhabiting a different time and space. Yet he knew that reality at this point was being with her.

The amusement park with its Ferris wheel and Octopus. He hadn't done that since he was a kid. The shooting gallery. Miniature grand prix racing with Lynne pressing, then passing him, as they raced the cars around the track. Nudie's Country & Western Outfitters—for Lynne, a sparkling white glittering stage outfit, all sequins and leather from boots to Stetson. Horses at Griffith Park. And then the long rides in the Apache back to the trailer park before he drove away to the emptiness of his rooms.

Philo was parked by the door of the Palomino, waiting for her. The radio played softly. It was still early and the sound of the band inside dimly reached him through the Palomino's double-thick doors. They opened. Lynne stepped out, the music louder now, then soft again as the door swung shut behind her. She looked around. Then, seeing Philo, she moved slowly to the Apache.

At the rear of the parking lot, an International Travelall cranked into life. Behind the wheel a shadowy figure watched and waited as Lynne climbed into Philo's truck. The lights of the Travelall flicked on as Philo pulled away. Moving out onto Lankersheim, the Travelall followed.

Lynne was quiet, subdued, sitting stiffly on the seat. Since entering the truck she hadn't said a word. She stared at her hands and then out the window at the night sky. Philo waited. She didn't look at him.

"You okay?" he asked finally.

She nodded. "I'm all right." Her voice was strained.

Philo waited a moment before speaking again. "A bad house tonight?"

"I'm all right, Philo!" Her voice was abrupt and cold and distant. She still hadn't looked at him.

He hit the straight stretch of highway past Tuxford and pushed the Apache to fifty. Behind him the Travelall moved up, closing, its high beams dazzling. Philo blinked at the bright lights shining in his eyes from the rear-view mirror.

"Somebody seems to want my attention," he said. He moved to the outside lane, maintaining speed.

The Travelall changed lanes with him, now directly behind and gaining. Philo pushed on the accelerator, increasing speed. The Travelall came on, closing the gap, accelerating. The Apache was hitting fifty-five when Philo felt the jolt. The Travelall had rammed him. The Apache fishtailed as Philo fought for control. He straightened the truck out and floored it. The Travelall did the same.

"I don't like the way that man's drivin'," said Philo. He swerved as the Travelall came alongside, then dropped back. It moved up again, this time ramming Philo's fender, knocking the Apache onto the shoulder of the road. Dust and gravel spurted as Philo fought the wheel. He edged back onto the highway; the Travelall pulled alongside. Philo squinted into the darkness, trying to catch a glimpse of the driver. He dropped back. In the moonlight, Philo caught the blue glint of steel. Doublebarrels peeked through the Travelall's window.

"Get down!" he yelled.

Lynne, white-faced, dropped to the floor. Philo cut the wheel sharply, ramming the side of the Travelall. The wagon careened across the road, its rear end sliding. Then a flash and a roar as both barrels of the shotgun went off. Chunks of glass cascaded onto the Apache. The driver of the Travelall had blown out his own windshield. Out of control, the Travelall spun crazily across the roadway, finally coming to rest in a ditch.

Jamming on his brakes, Philo brodied around and floored it. The Travelall, its lights pointing into the field by the side of the road, sat motionless. Philo looked back. It didn't follow.

Lynne crawled onto the seat. Wide-eyed with fright, she hugged her knees, shivering.

Philo slowed the Apache as they cut down a side street and onto another arterial. "Somebody you know?" he asked, his lips a hard, thin line.

Lynne nodded, desolate. "Schyler."

"I thought you said he didn't care."

Her voice, almost a whisper. "He must have changed his mind." She stared into the darkness. Philo nodded. There really wasn't too much more to say.

He pulled into the trailer court, cutting his engine and lights fifty yards from Lynne's trailer. The Apache rolled to a stop. He looked at her. She was sitting against the far door still hugging her knees and crying softly. A wave of tenderness swept over him. He relaxed, seeing the little girl in her, frightened and unhappy.

"What is it?" he asked.

"I'm scared." Her eyes flicked past his face.

He moved toward her, protective. "I won't let nothin' happen to you."

She choked back a sob. "That's not what . . ." she caught her breath. ". . . not what I'm afraid of." She looked at him, pleading. Silently sobbing.

Philo waited.

"I'm afraid for Schyler. Please don't hurt him." She wiped at her eyes, snuffling.

Jesus, thought Philo, feeling a stab of pain as the anger rose in him again. He turned away from her, trying to control himself. "That sonofabitch tried to blow my head off. He didn't even care if you were next to me!" Philo was a confused mass of thoughts. It was difficult sorting it all out while Lynne was pleading for the guy who just tried to kill him.

"That's just it," said Lynne, composing herself. "He wasn't trying to do any more than scare you. He don't even know how to shoot."

"I don't like the way he was tryin' to find out," said Philo. He turned back to her.

"I know him, Philo." She grabbed his hand with both of hers. "He's probably in there hiding. Scared out of his wits."

Philo looked at her. Her eyes welled up with tears. He smoothed her hair. "Sure hate to see you cry."

"Let me talk to him. Please." Her eyes were still pleading.

Philo looked down at his hands. "I don't know," he said.

Lynne moved closer to him. She put her arms around his neck. All honey and warmth. "Please . . . for me."

Philo hesitated, then relented. "While you're talking," he said, "tell him that I want you to come with me. I want you to stay with me."

"Oh Philo." Her lips reached for his. He tasted the saltiness of her tears. Laying her head on his shoulder, she wept.

Holding her, he reached into the glove compartment and withdrew the manilla envelope. "Now you just stop them tears," he said, "that's what I want." He gently wiped her eyes with his thumb and handed her the envelope. "Hold onto this."

Lynne opened the envelope and looked. The two thousand. "Oh no," she said, "I couldn't. I . . ."

"Yes, you can," said Philo, closing her hand over the money. "I'm tellin' you to."

She stared at him with love and bewilderment. Her lip quivered, eyes welling. She threw her arms around him.

"Don't want to see you cry no more." He held her close.

Orville crawled beneath the '48 Chevy pick-up. Within reach of his arm were a box of tools, an acetylene torch, and two cold beers. Orville was a firm believer in mixing business with pleasure. The tow truck was parked fifteen feet away, its radio tuned to Triple A calls. The truck was Orville's only link with the economy. With it, he earned enough to keep himself in beer and gas by rescuing distressed motorists well before their official Triple A truck arrived on the scene. It was an effective if not lucrative way of keeping himself off the job market.

The '48 Chevy was up on blocks. He took a slug of beer from the bottle and lit the acetylene torch. Pulling a pair of goggles over his eyes, Orville crept back under the battered truck.

Through a crack in the door of the shed Clyde watched Orville, fascinated. The bright tip of the torch flame appealed to the ape's sense of the unusual, the bright sparks and hot metal to his sense of beauty. In short, he was curious. Crooking a finger through the crack where door met jamb, he grabbed the chain with its new lock. With one great jerk, he pulled chain, lock, and hinge off the outside door. Tossing the hardware aside, he exited the shed. Rolling over to where Orville was working, Clyde squatted down on his haunches, peering beneath the truck, delighted with the sparks dropping from the frame to the ground below. Waiting for some sort of recognition from the prone Orville, he helped himself to a beer. He drained it in one gulp.

Orville stopped the torch and reached from beneath the truck for a beer. His hand closed around four hairy knuckles instead.

"Clyde, you sonofabitch, how'd you get out?" Orville glared at the ape. Clyde returned the stare. Taking a pull from the empty can, Clyde shook it, peered into the innards, then dropped it as useless on the ground. He turned to the second can just as Orville, divining the ape's intentions, whipped off his goggles and grabbed the remaining beer from under the reaching arm of the Man of the Forest.

Clyde, somewhat put out by Orville's action, showed his displeasure by picking the truck up off its blocks and rocking it. As the blocks fell, Orville flattened himself to the ground. He looked up at Clyde, horrified. He was afraid to give Clyde the beer for fear he'd drop the truck, and terrified not to give it to him for fear he'd drop the truck.

"Goddamn you, Clyde . . . ." Orville was sweating like a pig.

Clyde shook the pickup. Orville turned green.

"Good boy, Clyde," quivered Orville. "Don't let go . . . you just keep holdin' this stinkin' truck."

The light of the Apache turned up the driveway and came to a stop, outlining Clyde. Philo jumped out and walked toward the ape. "What the hell you doin' Clyde?" he shouted.

Clyde looked toward Philo, grunted, and began shaking the truck like a toy. From beneath the '48, the plaintive voice of Orville rent the night.

"Philo, that you . . .? Call this sumbitch . . . Wait! Don't call him!"

The truck was rocking outrageously as Orville made his move. Heaving the can of beer high in the air, he hollered and rolled out from under the truck like a pinball out of the chute.

Clyde dropped the truck and grabbed for the beer, catching it with both hands. He had it upended and swallowed before Orville stopped rolling. The truck crashed down awesomely. In a state of near shock, Orville looked back at the spot where he had been lying.

"Dammit, Orville," said Philo, "I keep tellin' ya. I don't want you feedin' 'im no beer between meals."

SIX

It was morning, almost pretty on the Hollywood Freeway. There hadn't been time for the smog to settle. Philo and Orville cruised down the freeway in the tow truck listening to Mel Tillis on the portable. Orville was still talking about his near demise.

". . . Then the sumbitch had me shittin' under there for near fifteen minutes, 'fore you came."

A call came in over the jimmied two-way, directing Triple A to a flat somewhere ahead on the freeway. Orville checked his watch. "Hold on," he said, "we got one." He floored the rig.

A mile and a half later, Orville saw the crippled Buick sitting on the shoulder. Orville braked to a stop behind the disabled vehicle. He swung from the cab and approached the motorist, who was walking toward the truck. "See ya need some help," he said. Philo swung out of the other door of the truck.

"Glad you came by so quick," said the motorist with relief.

Orville grabbed his tools and in a matter of seconds had the car jacked up and the tyre removed. He rolled the spare from the man's trunk. "Ya know," he said to Philo, "Clyde's been actin' mighty strange lately. My guess is he's hornier than a three-peckered billy goat."

67

"Been wonderin' about that," said Philo.

The cars on the freeway whizzed by as Orville, all precision, cranked down the lug nuts on the wheel. "I mean he just don't sit there all day and think about Oreo cookies." Orville released the jack, dropped the car, and in the same motion tossed jack and tools into the back of the tow truck. He raised his arms, done. He coulda just finished roping and tying a calf. The whole thing had taken less than two minutes. "That'll be twelve dollars," he said to the motorist.

"What?" said the motorist. He looked at Orville, dumbfounded.

"That'll be twelve dollars," repeated Orville. "That's what I charge."

"But I called the auto club," said the motorist in confusion. "I thought you were the auto club."

"I didn't say nothin' about bein' the auto club." Orville was playing it straight. The man shook his head, not yet angry, but beginning to feel as though he had been had.

"Listen, mister," said Orville, "I got another call. I stopped only cause it seemed you needed help. Bein' as you made a mistake, I'm only gonna charge you ten dollars."

The man looked at Orville. "Well, that's mighty kind of you," he said doubtfully. He pulled a ten from his billfold and handed it to Orville.

Nodding thanks, Orville pocketed the money. The man stood there. He knew something just happened, but didn't quite know what it was. Orville and Philo jumped back into the tow truck. Orville checked his watch. As he pulled onto the freeway he could see the Triple A truck coming up in the rear-view. Another score for the good guys.

"All right!" said Orville, turning to Philo. "Let's eat."

An outrageous number of motorcycles were parked outside the small house in Pacoima. Inside, the living room, dining area, kitchen, and hallway were crammed with crates and boxes of TVs, radios, CBs, and sundry pieces of other people's property. Taking up what space remained were banners, posters, signs, and placards depicting black widows. The door from an exterminator's truck, black widow rampant, rested against a wall. Sprawled in and among the loot and insignia were the twelve members of the club, two of them in sorry shape. The muscular one who looked like Geronimo was talking, his face a mass of bumps and bruises.

"Shit," he said. "I never knowed anybody could hit so hard, or so fast." He tentatively rubbed his cheek, which was swollen to twice normal size.

Elmo, the faggoty-looking one, sporting a black eye and goose egg on his forehead, agreed emphatically. "He coulda been Denver Tank Murdoch."

Cholla, the leader of the Black Widows, a balding, beer-fat, jackbooted senior delinquent, turned to two other members of the group who were sprawled on chairs. "Sound like him?" He flipped the silk scarf from his belly with his riding crop. A tattooed black widow crawled above his naval.

Dallas, the ever-present steer horns on his head, shrugged. "I don't know," he said. "Didn't get to see him so close as Elmo." Woody, raising his eye patch, guffawed.

Elmo bristled. "Least I didn't drop my bike and run."

"Hell no," snapped Bruno, a tall, muscular Widow who flexed his biceps continuously, "you dropped Moose's bike." Bruno's forte was pumping iron whether or not the weights were actually present.

Dallas stood up, red-faced, and headed for Elmo. "Creep . . ."

"Sit your ass down," barked Cholla to the oncoming Dallas. The biker reluctantly returned to his seat, glaring at Elmo. Cholla continued. "Ain't it enough somebody else is kickin' shit outta ya without doin' it t' each other? If this is the same guy we're talkin' about, he 'pears to have a growin' collection of our motorcycles."

"We don't know for sure if he took 'em or not. We were . . . uh." Frank hesitated, picking morosely at the scab on his face.

"Unconscious for two hours." Dallas finished his sentence for him. The room broke into hysterics.

"Listen, motherfu . . ." Frank half rose from his chair.

Cholla intervened. "Would you assholes shut up." He motioned at the two to sit down. "First thing we do is find out who we're talkin' about. Then we see if he's the one took our bikes."

"How we gonna know where to find him?" chirped Elmo.

Cholla tapped his head, indicating superior knowledge and wisdom that set him apart from the other Widows. "Can't be too many guys in the valley, drive around with a fuckin' ape." He looked around. The rest of the bikers had always been impressed with Cholla's analytical mind. He smiled knowingly.

The Oxnard branch of the Department of Motor Vehicles was uncrowded. The tow truck rolled into the parking lot, Orville at the wheel, Ma Boggs beside him. She was holding tightly to the test she passed at the San Fernando Valley branch. She put the three other tests she'd failed over the visor.

"Don't 'spect I'll need these no more."

"Just take your time, Ma," cautioned Orville. "This is the easy part."

"Sure glad there ain't no more squiggly pictures" she rejoined.

Orville parked the truck, pulled up the emergency brake, and slid out of the cab. He helped Ma down and led her into the building. They headed directly for the line where a disinterested examiner was testing eyes; Ma held tightly to her test with the perfect score.

The tow truck rolled homeward, Orville silent behind the wheel. Ma stared out the window, her jaw set. Passing a billboard, she squinted and stuck her head forward, one hand held over her eye. A moment later she covered the other eye and squinted at another billboard, silently

70

mouthing the letters.

"Whyn't ya tell him that you wear glasses?" asked Orville after a moment.

"None a his goddamned business what I wear." Ma continued looking at the billboards, mumbling letters, then added, "Jest use 'em fer readin', anyway."

Orville drove on in silence, waiting. When nothing further was forthcoming from the old lady, he cocked his head at her. "What else?"

"Told me I was too old," she said reluctantly. "Asshole!"

The tow truck pulled into the driveway of their house and parked by the back door.

"Orville," said Ma.

"Yes, Ma."

She waited a beat. "Next time I'll wear m' glasses."

Philo combed his hair carefully, making sure each strand was in place. He observed himself in the mirror, rubbing at a spot on his cheek. He sang slightly off key, to the melody from the radio, humming the words he didn't know. He flicked off the radio, checked himself once again in the mirror, and smiled. Lookin' good and feelin' great. He turned off the light and moved through the kitchen and out the door, headed for the shed.

Unlocking the chain, he entered Clyde's quarters. The ape was sitting in a corner meditating. Philo nudged him once to get his attention, then went to a cabinet and removed a large brush from one of the shelves. Clyde grunted amiably as Philo began combing out the tangles in the long red hair. Clyde lifted his arm to allow Philo to attack the matted area on his side, his eyes rolled back with pleasure at the attention. When Philo finished, he gently pinched Clyde's huge black cheeks and looked deep into his brown eyes. "God, you're a handsome devil," he said.

Scratching the ape's head, Philo led the acquiescent Clyde to the Apache. They both climbed in, and moved out down the road.

71

"Now, Clyde," Philo warned his aboriginal companion, "we're goin' to meet a *lady*, so I want you to handle it." The ape looked at him with adoration. "That means no fartin', spittin', pissin', or pickin' at your ass."

Clyde put an arboreal arm around Philo's shoulders.

"Cause if you do, I'll kick shit outta you on the spot."

Clyde grunted, his teeth bared happily as Philo tousled his head.

When they reached the trailer park, Philo checked himself once more in the rear-view. Yes, sir, he sure was a fine-lookin' fella. He checked Clyde for any sign of disarray, then turned into the entrance and headed down Row No. 3. Clyde bounced off the window as Philo jammed on the brakes.

Lynne Halsey-Taylor's trailer was gone!

Philo backed up to make sure he hadn't gone down the wrong row, his heart racing. No mistake. An empty space stood where the trailer had been. Backing up with a squeal of tyres, Philo stopped the Apache beside the shack with the neon sign reading OFFICE. He jumped out and pounded on the door. Getting no response, Philo pounded again. The shuffle of footsteps, and a mumbled "I'm comin', I'm comin'." He waited impatiently, to sounds of fumbling and muttered curses. Finally the door opened. An old pensioner, half drunk, was stuffing his false teeth into his mouth.

"Where's the trailer that was in that spot over there?" Philo demanded.

The old man finished adjusting his teeth and looked at Philo, bleary-eyed His breath reeked. "Hmmph . . ." he peered at Philo. "What spot?"

"Over there," said Philo, grabbing the old man's arm and pointing.

"The old man squinted into the darkness seeing nothing and caring less. "Don't see it" he said.

"Over there!" said Philo. He jabbed his finger in exasperation at the empty space.

"That's row No. 3!" stated the pensioner triumphantly.

"Where is it?"

"Spot No. 5," declared the pensioner matter-of-factly. "Trailer's gone."

"I know it's gone, goddamnit!" shouted Philo. "Where did she go?"

"Back home, I s'pect," said the pensioner, shaking free of Philo's grip.

"Denver?" Philo looked at the old man.

"I dunno," said the pensioner, "some folks just won' take me 't' their conf'dence. Plates said Colorado. Sound right t'you?"

Philo was losing patience. "When did they leave?"

"Lemme think." The old man scratched his head in perplexity. "What time is it?"

"Near eight."

"They lef' this morning." The old man scrunched up his jaw, agreeing with himself. "Yep, they lef' this morning."

Philo left the old man standing in the doorway with bugs flitting about his head.

"An' goo'by d' you." The old man stared at the receding taillights, then tottered back to the interior of the shack, removed his false teeth, and dropped them into an empty glass.

Pushing the Apache to sixty-five, Philo made it to the Palomino in record time. He squealed into the lot, cut the ignition, set the brake, and was out the door before the engine died. "Be right back," he yelled at Clyde. The ape pounded on the door in acknowledgment.

He ran across the lot and into the club, pushing past the man collecting the cover. Philo looked around angrily.

Onstage a band was playing. The place was packed. Philo's eyes darted over the crowd, half expecting to see her.

"Hey, Philo!"

He turned around. The bartender was motioning to him. Philo walked to the bar and leaned across it.

"Got a message for you," said the bartender.

"What is it?"

The bartender reached into his shirt pocket and pulled out a folded piece of paper. He handed it to Philo.

Philo opened the note slowly. He held it to the light. It was short, sweet, and to the point. "DEAR PHILO. I GOTTA GO. I'M SORRY — LYNNE HALSEY-TAYLOR."

Philo read the note and then, as if not sure of the words, read it again. Then, angrily, he crumpled it into a ball and threw it down. Philo turned around, eyes unseeing, conscious only of his anger and frustration. The note, forcefully thrown, landed in the drink of a man at the table behind him. It splattered his drink onto his immaculately pressed outfit.

The man, Putnam, a cartoon of self-importance with no sense of humour, jerked back with an oath, dabbing at himself with a napkin. Furious, he jumped up from his chair and glared at Philo.

"Whyn't cha watch what the hell you're doin'?"

"Whyn't cha get stuffed?" said Philo, turning to leave.

Herb, a black man, Putnam's companion, stuck his foot into the aisle behind Philo. He smiled and winked at his partner.

"Hold on there, cowboy," said Putnam. He grabbed Philo's arm and shoved.

Tripping over Herb's foot, Philo went down, landing with a thump on the hard wooden floor. Putnam, Herb, and their two tablemates laughed. A monumental mistake in judgment; the wrong place, the wrong time, and the wrong person.

Philo erupted off the floor like a volcano. The table the four had been sitting at flew ten feet, crashing in a splintered pile by the jukebox. Putnam's smile disintegrated into a rosy mish-mosh of chipped teeth and split gums as Philo's knuckles rearranged his features. Herb, half out of his chair, screamed for help, and before Philo descended upon him found refuge under the nearest table. One of the other men picked up a chair and demolished it across Philo's shoulders. He shrugged it off and returned with an uppercut

74

that sent the man flying across two tables. Their occupants immediately joined the battle.

By this time a dozen people were punching and stomping each other with joyful abandon. Bodies, teeth, glasses, chairs, and dinners were flying everywhere. A bottle whistled past Philo's ear to splatter against the wall. Philo picked up the thrower and heaved him down the bar, clearing it of glasses, ashtrays, and customers.

The melee moved onto the dance floor as dancers collapsed in screaming, kicking piles, knocked down by sliding, stumbling combatants. The band played on.

A gorilla of a man leaped onto the stage, only to be felled by a Fender guitar, which the lead guitarist brought crashing down on his head. The sounds coming from the speakers were unbelievable.

Two grinning giants bore down on Philo wielding bottles. He stopped them both cold.

Onstage, the drummer beat a tattoo with his sticks on the head of a comatose patron. The speakers tumbled onto the dance floor. Philo shook off an attacker who was unceremoniously attached to his back by dumping him head first into a woofer.

Above the din, Philo heard the sound of approaching sirens. Without doubt it was time to leave. Philo looked at the bartender. "Somebody call the cops?"

The bartender ducked a flying bottle. He gulped. "Those guys you were beatin' on, Philo . . . they *are* the cops!"

"Shit!" said Philo. He clubbed his way to the door past prostrate forms. Behind him the battle was still going strong.

Outside the Palomino, Philo stood for a moment in the cool air. He took a deep breath. A guy and his date were standing outside the club listening to the carnage within.

"What's happening in there?" asked the guy apprehensively.

"It's the happy hour," said Philo confidentially. "They're just runnin' a little bit over."

75

It was midmorning. Orville sat at the back door watching Philo attach the camper top to the bed of the Apache. Clyde hunted crickets in the struggling lawn.

"She didn't say where she was goin'?" Orville asked.

Philo hammered at a clamp with the heel of his hand. "Nope," he said.

"Well, how d'ya know where to look?" Orville picked at his nose reflectively, then hoisted himself off the stoop to help Philo with the top.

"I know," said Philo.

Orville pushed down on the shell as Philo clamped it into place. "How d'ya know she wants you to come after her?" he asked.

"Orville," said Philo, "you're asking them dumb questions again."

Orville, chagrined, methodically tightened a bolt. "Ya takin' Clyde?" he asked.

"Yup," Philo wrenched down the nut on the bolt Orville was holding.

Orville looked at Philo from the corner of his eye. "Got room for one more?"

Philo looked up and smiled. "Yup."

"EEEyyoo," Orville yelled. "Here I come!" He dropped the pliers and ran into the house to pack his gear. A second later his head popped out of the door. "Jes' which way is it we're goin'?"

"East," said Philo.

"Seems reasonable." Orville zipped back into the house as Ma Boggs made her way around the corner. She contemplated Philo as he put the finishing touches on the camper shell and began loading his gear.

"What about the baboon?" She ran a bony finger through her stringy hair.

"Orangutan, Ma, Clyde's an orangutan."

"What's the difference?"

"Ribs." Philo tossed his bedroll into the shell.

"Eh?"

"Other apes have more ribs. Clyde has twelve pair. Just like you and me." Philo heaved in a large coil of rope.

"What're ya gonna do with 'im?"

"Comin' with me," said Philo, helping Clyde into the camper.

Ma Boggs regarded him with a biased eye. "When ya comin' back?"

Orville stumbled out of the back door of the house, bedroll in hand. It had taken him less than a minute to get ready.

"When ya comin' back?" repeated Ma, louder this time, to include Orville.

"Soon as it's time, Ma," said Orville. He tossed his roll into the back of the Apache. Philo started it up.

The old lady looked at her son and Philo perversely. The truck pulled out of the driveway. "Don't seem right . . .," she grumbled. "Leave an old lady alone . . ." She turned in the direction of the Apache. "What about m' goddamn licence?" she shouted. The Apache was halfway down the block. She turned back to the house, muttering. "All alone in a big ol' house . . . not even a *dog* fer company . . . humph . . . twelve ribs . . . don't believe any a' that shit . . .!"

SEVEN

Early morning, the sun just beginning to top the San Gabriels. A candy apple purple dune buggy turned off Sunset Boulevard at Pacific Coast Highway, made a right, then zipped around the chain-link barrier to the beach. Putnam, his face swollen behind mirrored sunglasses, a plaster covering his nose, pulled to a stop. "We're here," he said, ponderously stating the obvious.

Herb, totally unmarked, dressed for the beach in plaids and stripes, nodded as the two men exited the vehicle. Rummaging in the rear of the buggy, Putnam handed his partner miscellaneous pieces of gear, an ice chest, beach blankets, shovel, and an intriguing-looking instrument consisting of a long metal rod with a disc attached to one end.

Fully loaded, Herb uncomfortably followed Putnam across the lot and down to the beach.

"Guess this is all right," said Putnam, pointing to a spot in the sand. Herb gratefully divested himself of his burden as Putnam picked up the strange apparatus. He flicked a switch and peered hopefully at the meter attached to the end of the rod.

"You wouldn't believe the shit I find with this thing, Herb," he said.

"No kidding," said Herb. He picked up the shovel and rested it on his shoulder.

"Two weeks ago," said Putnam, "I found a pocket knife, three quarters, and an airplane."

"An airplane?"

"A toy, asshole." Putnam held the disc over a spot in the sand and hunkered down to look at the meter.

"How often you come here?" asked Herb. He watched his partner tapping the dial.

"Every week." Putnam stood up and continued down the beach; the magic, somethin'-for-nothin', metal-detector wand weaving its mystic circles above the sand.

"Whatcha looking for this week?"

"You putting me on?" Putnam tapped the meter again.

"Naw," said Herb. He dropped the spade end of the shovel as he walked, creating crescents in the sand.

"You don't look for anything in particular," said Putnam. "You just look. You never know what you're gonna find."

"But how come you gotta come out so early?" Herb twirled the shovel.

"Cause the goddamn tractor comes and turns all the good shit under if ya don't." Putnam swung the detector in a wide arc. "There could be a fortune right under our feet and without this we'd never know it."

"No kidding!" said Herb.

Suddenly the needle on the meter jumped erratically, bouncing back and forth.

"Hey, there you go, Putnam!" yelled Herb in excitement. "You got somethin'. You got somethin'." He dropped the shovel and pointed at the box on the handle.

"Hold on, now," said Putnam, "Let me get the hottest spot." He moved the machine back and forth, watching the needle, then stepped to the place that showed the most action. "Right here," he said. "Dig right on this spot. This is it."

Herb, hardly able to contain himself, began to dig feverishly. After a dozen or so shovelfuls, he stopped and looked at his partner.

"Looks like it's deep," said Putnam, removing his sunglasses, his black eye swelling with purple.

Herb began digging again, working up a sweat, totally engrossed on the treasure just a few shovels away.

"Well, Herb," said Putnam, opening a Coke, "what we gonna do about that sonofabitch?"

Herb stopped, out of breath. He spit on his hands and rested against the shovel. "Don't know what we can do." He kicked at the sand. "We weren't on duty. . . and we did sort of provoke him."

Putnam sat down, smoothing the sand. "You mean to tell me you'd let him get away with it?"

"What you got in mind?"

"What I got in mind," said Putnam, "is to break his stupid head."

Herb began digging again, tossing shovelful after shovelful onto the large pile accumulating above him. "You sure that thing works?"

"I'm sure," said Putnam.

"You don't even know where to find him." Herb paused.

"I'll find him." Putnam picked up a handful of sand and let it dribble through his fingers.

"You mean you'd spend your two weeks' medical leave lookin' for 'im?" Herb leaned back against the growing pit.

"I'll spend the next two years lookin' for him if I have to."

Herb picked up the shovel, digging more. Sweat dripped from his ebony skin. "I dunno, maybe we oughta just forget him."

"Forget him!" said Putnam, jumping to his feet. "I'd sooner forget my pension. Besides, I got an idea. It didn't take a whole lot to provoke him, now, did it?"

Herb shook his head. "Uh-uh!"

"Well," Putnam's face broke into a smile, "next time it'll be different. I got a plan."

The shovel clunked against something hard buried in the pit.

"Hey," yelled Herb. "I've got it! I've got it!"

Putnam jumped into the hole, tossing the shovel out of the way. On hands and knees he scrabbled in the sand. He pulled. Too heavy. Grabbing the shovel, he stuck it under the object and pried.

"Gimme a hand!"

Herb joined him in the pit, scraping away the sand to get a fingerhold. The object moved. Together the two men pulled, slowly breaking it loose.

"It's coming!" yelled Herb. "It's coming!"

Putnam, his face florid with excitement, pushed Herb away. He grabbed under the treasure with both hands, straining mightily.

Herb stood in hushed expectancy, waiting. Then with a mighty heave, Putnam jerked the object from the ground. He stood up slowly, turning to Herb in disgust. He dropped it in the sand and stared. Staring back through its naked and rusting threads was a decomposing steel-belted tyre.

It was noon when Cholla and eleven other Black Widows filed out of the house in Pacoima. They mounted their choppers; Frank and Elmo, machineless, climbed on behind two others. The ten bikes rolled south, falling into formation with Cholla in the lead. Heads turned and teenie boppers waved as Cholla assumed the appropriate riding stance. The pack was on the run.

The bikers pulled into the parking lot of the Palomino, reining up with pomp and precision. They cut their engines, and with final bursts dismounted as Cholla ceremoniously parked his bike. The others milled about, waiting. Elmo, having adjusted his hat to the correct angle, and hunching his body into his most menacing stance, stalked toward the building. As he passed Cholla, the bikers froze. Midstride Cholla's riding crop stopped Elmo cold. He turned, reddening, and realizing his indiscretion, sheepishly returned to the fold. Cholla, generous as are all great leaders, smiled beatifically and strode forward, taking his place at the head of the tribe. The search for Philo had begun.

Route 66 moves cross country from Los Angeles, a black ribbon of highway that once carried the mainstream of east-west traffic. But since the construction of the interstates, it carries those preferring a more leisurely and colourful drive.

The Apache travelled east, past small wineries, dairy farms, and fruit orchards. Groves of orange trees lined the road between vacant gas stations, rundown motels, and faded cafes, casualties of the freeway that ran parallel and several miles south.

A roadside stand, abundant with fruits and vegetables, came up on the left. A car waited for service in the parking area. Philo eased on the brake and pulled in. Orville, asleep in the passenger seat, jolted awake as the Apache bumped up the drive and came to a halt.

"Mmm . . . What's up?" he asked groggily.

"Pit stop," said Philo, opening his door and stepping out.

Orville jumped down and they walked to the stand.

The harried girl at the scale was desperately trying to please a customer. The fat, red-haired lady seemed to find fault with everything. The girl placed a sack on the scale.

"No," said the lady peevishly, "I think I'll take a quarter of a pound."

"But they only cost a quarter a pound," said the girl.

"But all I want is a quarter of a pound." The lady glared, tapping her foot.

The girl sighed and removed two tomatoes from the bag. The sack tottered for a moment, then slid off the scale, dropping to the ground with a splat. The girl picked up the bag and looked inside. Shaking her head, she emptied the bag into a garbage can. Looking up, she saw Orville.

"I'd like a different bag," said the lady. Nobody was going to put anything past her.

Orville watched the process, his eyes twinkling. The girl, wind-blown and sparkling fresh, was definitely put together.

She reached under the counter for another bag. Orville winked at her, then seriously approached the lady from behind. He leaned down and whispered in her ear.

The lady reared back, shocked. "Well . . . well, I never!" Waddling away quickly, she rubbed talcum all' the way to her Dart.

The girl beamed at Orville, relieved. "May I help *you*?" she asked.

"Shor' can," said Orville. He leaned forward and stared into her eyes.

At the other side of the stand, the man waiting on Philo silently quartered an orange and handed it to him. Philo nodded thanks and carried the wedges to the rear of the truck. He offered one to the hairy hand that protruded from the shell. The wedge was withdrawn, sniffed, and returned uneaten.

Returning to the stand, Philo chose another type of orange and motioned for the man to quarter it. Back to the camper. This time it disappeared, peel and all. Philo walked back to the stand and bought five pounds.

Orville had filled several bags with his orders. He was buying anything and everything the girl suggested.

"What's your name?" he asked, still staring at her.

"Echo," she looked up, giving him a friendly sidelong glance.

"Huh?"

"Echo," she repeated it slowly.

"Oh."

"How about some cantaloupes?" She held up two beauties.

Orville couldn't keep his eyes off her body, swelling out the cotton dress. "Beautiful," he murmured.

"How many?" asked Echo.

Orville didn't even hear the question. "You live around here?"

She smiled. "Down past the wash. Left at the Broken Arrow Trading Post and six miles to Piute Junction."

"Where's the wash?"

"How come you want to know 'bout me?"

Orville licked his lips thoughtfully, his eyes never leaving her face. "Cuz I never seen no one made me feel like you do, right outta the gate."

Echo looked at him long and hard. "Where you headed?" she asked.

Philo returned to the truck and stuffed a couple of sacks behind the seat. He slid in as Echo, carrying a large purse and two sacks, approached the passenger side. She put her sacks next to Philo's and got in. Orville climbed in after her and closed the door. Philo looked at them. He waited. They stared straight ahead. Finally he started the truck and pulled onto the highway.

Silence. The truck sped down the roadway. No one spoke. Orville and Echo stared into the distance ahead. Philo glanced over at them, then reached back out the window and knocked on the camper shell.

The silence disturbed Echo. Nervously, she turned and looked at nothing outside Orville's window. Five hairy fingers reached through the curtain and handed Philo a can of open beer. He drank it slowly, then reached into a sack for something to eat. He withdrew a tomato, then put it back. Swiftly, Echo handed him a peach. An offering. She eyed the beer in Philo's hand, which seemed to have miraculously appeared out of nowhere.

Philo took the peach, wiped it on his shirt, and took a bite. "What's your name?" he asked.

"Echo."

"Huh?" Philo took another bite of peach.

"Echo."

"Oh."

From the back of the truck there came a loud thump. Echo looked around in surprise. The Apache hit a pothole in the road. Another thump. Echo, satisfied, turned to Orville.

"Orville, what you tell that lady that made her stomp

away so fast?"

Orville laughed, "I told her that you had the clap."

The Apache drove all day, stopping only for gas. Night found it climbing into the foothills. Orville and Echo dozed as the truck pushed on, its headlights punching through the wall of blackness. A sign off the shoulder of the road flashed in the glare of the high beams: CAMP-GROUND ONE MILE AHEAD.

Philo eased off the throttle, searching ahead in the darkness for the turnoff. An arrow pointing down a dirt road told him where. He pulled off the highway and turned in to the campground. Finding a vacant space, Philo backed in. Orville and Echo were still asleep. Philo climbed out of the cab, closed the door quietly, and made his way to the back of the truck. He opened the rear of the camper. Clyde happily tumbled out and disappeared into the bush, eager for some space and a chance to hunt up some grubs.

Philo gathered kindling, made a fire, put on dinner, and laid out the bedrolls. Then, preparations for the night completed, he woke Orville and Echo. They stumbled yawning from the cab of the Apache.

"It ain't a Scotty's cheeseburger," said Phillo, "but chow's on."

"Well, lookit you," Orville looked around in appreciation. "Doin' all that."

"Ya'll looked so pretty, I couldn't bear wakin' ya." Philo grinned.

"I'm starving," voiced Echo. She checked out the pot steaming on the grate and helped herself to a bowlful.

"It's just chili and tortillas," said Philo, "and some tortillas and tortillas."

"Ya know," said Orville, digging into the pot, "ya can't expect to whip Tank Murdoch on these damn tortillas."

"We ain't gonna swap recipes, Orville." Phillo rolled himself a burrito.

Echo, her mouth full, popped into the conversation.

88

"Who's Tank Murdoch?"

"Well," Orville's face became as serious as you can get with a mouthful of chili, "if you don't know, somebody's sadly neglected your education."

Ma Boggs was in the kitchen, her bony hands engaged in frying hot dogs in a heavy iron skillet. They curled and crackled, sputtering lard. She mumbled to herself, pushing at the skinny wieners with a wooden spoon.

A police cruiser pulled up the driveway, its lights shining onto the front porch of the house. It pulled to a stop. Putnam and Herb emerged. They walked to the door. Herb pushed the bell, waited a few moments, then pushed it again.

"I'm comin', I'm comin', goddamnit!" Ma wiped her hands on her dress and went to the door. She opened it a crack and peered out. "Who is it?" she asked.

"It's the police," said Herb.

The door opened a little farther. "What you want with an ol' lady?" Ma squinted at Herb's face, which blended into the darkness behind him.

"We're looking for a Philo Beeddoe," said Putnam, officially. "Beddoe," corrected Herb.

"Beddoe," Putnam went on. "Our records say that he lives at this address."

"Well, your records are wrong." Ma continued to squitn at Herb. "He lives at the address in the back. What's he done?"

Putnam, in his best Joe Friday manner, looked at her sternly. "We're just lookin' for him, ma'am."

"Well, he ain't here no more. He's gone off."

Herb and Putnam looked at each other.

"Took that sumbitch Clyde with 'im," Ma continued.

"Clyde?" Putnam leaned forward.

"His ape."

"His ape?" They looked at Ma and then at each other.

"You heard me. What you makin' me repeat m'self fer?"

"Do you know where he's gone?" Herb asked politely.

"Who gives a shit?" said Ma. "Stealin' all my Oreos. Crappin' all over the place. Twelve pair a' ribs my ass!"

Putnam and Herb looked at each other again and simultaneously began to back off the porch.

"Thank you, ma'am," mumbled Herb, "Sorry t' bother ya." Putnam stumbled into the bushes.

"I'm sorry too," grumbled Ma. "Leavin' a ol' lady t' fend fer herself . . . needin' pertecshun." She called after the rapidly retreating patrol car, "Don't seem right . . . no it don't . . . every goddamn cookie . . .!"

The fire had burned low, shadows were dancing on Echo's face. Orville watched her. They had finished eating and were having coffee as Philo tinkered under the hood of the Apache.

"I don't suppose there's a ladies' room hereabouts," said Echo.

"There's lots of 'em. Take your pick." Orville waved his arm expansively.

Echo nodded and wandered off to find a suitable spot.

"Whatcha doin'?" said Orville.

"Gonna be hittin' some high country." Philo wiped his hands. He called out, "Thought I'd adjust the carburettor."

Orville nodded absently. "She shor is sumthin' else, ain't she?"

Philo looked over his shoulder. "She sure is. You're just full of surprises."

"Appreciate your making her feel t' home," said Orville sincerely.

A blood-curdling scream issued from the depths of the chaparral. Philo and Orville turned as one and stared into the darkness.

"Oh shit," said Philo, hitting his head with his palm.

"Clyde?" asked Orville, starting to his feet.

"Sounds like it."

The violent crashing and thrashing in the brush were

terrible. A moment later Echo stumbled into the campsite, white with fear. She snatched up her purse and grabbed hold of Orville. Terrified and breathless, she struggled to get the words out.

"There's . . . there's something horrible out there. My God . . . a monster . . . it's not a bear . . . I swear it, it's not even a *bear* . . .!" She was shaking uncontrollably.

From the darkness, the crashing came closer. Echo looked around, her eyes wide. She clutched at Orville. Then Clyde came into the clearing. He looked like a reincarnation of King Kong in the firelight. Happy to have found Philo, he ambled toward them. Echo screamed again, several times. Clyde looked at her, puzzled. Madly fumbling in her purse, Echo withdrew a tiny automatic. With shaking hands, she aimed it.

"Put that damn thing away and quiet down," said Philo forcefully. "It's only Clyde. You'll scare him."

Echo reluctantly lowered the weapon. "I'll scare *him*!"

"Shh," said Philo. "C'mere, Clyde."

Clyde shuffled over to Philo and put an arm around his shoulder. He looked at Philo, then at Echo, hurt showing in his dark, soft eyes. He *had* been frightened.

Philo turned to Echo. "Come on over here 'n' I'll introduce you."

Not sure what she'd gotten into by her spur-of-the-moment decision, Echo, holding tightly to Orville's arm, gingerly approached Clyde.

Echo stared at the ape, who returned her look dolefully.

"Clyde, this is Echo."

"Hu?" grunted Clyde.

"Uh," said Clyde.

Dawn. The campground silent. As the sun topped the hills, Philo squirmed in his bag. He opened one eye, yawned, then fell back to sleep. Orville and Echo were curled, a large ball, in one bedroll. The embers of the fire cracked and smoldered gently.

Fifty yards away the engine of a Travelall turned over, purring quietly. Warming up. Then, with a quiet shifting of gears, the Travellall moved out of the campground, a familiar trailer behind it.

The afternoon sun beat on the San Fernando Valley. The air was sultry. Ma Boggs sat in her rocker dozing on the porch, an old blanket spread across her lap. She slapped halfheartedly at the gnats and no-see-ums flitting around her head, rocking gently. Her reverie was interrupted by the staccato roar of a dozen motorcycles. They rolled up the driveway, a mass of chrome, wheels, and unkempt bodies. Black Widows screeched across the sparse lawn, churning up clumps of dirt, leaving tyre tracks in the petunias. The bikes roared past the shed, three or four skidding to a halt next to Philo's digs. The bikers jumped off, running to the door, banging on it heavily. A couple of others leaped off their choppers and happily scrounged and pillaged among the wrecked cars, whooping and hollering and generally raising hell. Cholla, aloof to the depredations of his brood, rode majestically up to the porch. He gunned his machine imperiously.

"Hey, old lady," he leaned forward and shouted in her ear. "Where's Philo Beddoe?"

A three-wheeler with a VW engine rolled up next to the porch, Elmo cackling uproariously. He grinned at Cholla and peeled out, taking half a small garden with him.

"How the hell do I know?" glared Ma. She raised her voice, irritated at the intrusion. "Get offa my porch with that thing. Get offa my propity!"

Cholla grinned. "Not very hospitable."

Ma surveyed the havoc around her. "Hospitable my ass." The old lady glared at Cholla. "Git off my porch."

"If you insist," said Cholla, nodding to the nearest Widow and tossing him a chain. The biker wound one end around a pillar of the porch. He smiled at Ma and hooked the other end of the chain to Cholla's bike. Kicking the chopper into gear, Cholla roared off, pulling the post with him. With a wrenching crash, the pillar broke free, and half the roof broke with it. Cholla rode chortling across the lawn, dragging the pillar triumphantly.

Ma finally had enough. "I tol' ya," she bellowed.

The old lady threw off the comforter and pulled a twelve-gauge shotgun from her lap that she hadn't pulled a trigger on for forty years. She brought the pump to her shoulders and pointed it in the general direction of the scrambling Widows. She pulled one off. The recoil almost blew her off the rocker. The Widows, stunned, leaped for their machines, frantically kicking them into life. They fishtailed, spun, and swerved, trying to put distance between themselves and the smoking barrels, which blasted at them from everywhere. Ma pulled the pump again and blammed off another round. This one caught a chopper square in the gas tank, blowing it apart, sending the rider six feet into the air. The explosion set off another bike's tank, the Harley disintegrating into a jumble of parts and wheels. Another Widow crashed into a tree, while one more, racing to get out of there, damn near decapitated himself on the clothesline. Ma continued to blast away. Hell, this was almost fun. She took a bead on the three-wheeler and Elmo rose with a scream, grabbing at his ass as the pellets rattled about him. Bikeless Widows jumped onto those machines still mobile, hanging on for livin', as their drivers roared across the burning and smoking lawn. One chopper, with a sidecar, in a frenzy to escape, crashed into two half-filled garbage cans, dragging them clattering down the street, leaving a trail of trash behind it. Ma surveyed the desolation. Bits and pieces of bikes scattered everywhere; smoke, flames and destruction. She turned to her front door.

"Lotta goddamn nerve." She carried the gun like a dead chicken. "First the police, now this . . . I tol' them boys not to leave a vunnerbul ol' lady alone . . . hospitable . . . horseshit!"

93

EIGHT

Albuquerque, New Mexico. Country music singing from the speakers as the Apache rolled into town. Orville, Philo, and Echo sang and laughed along.

"Hey," said Philo. "I got an idea."

"What is it? What is it? What is it?" Echo ran the questions together like a machine gun.

"Bein'," said Philo, "as it's hotter 'n' dustier than a horny toad's belly, and bein' as everybody in this truck is beginnin' to smell as bad as Clyde, what say we spring for a motel and a hot shower?"

"Yaaaayyy," shouted Orville and Echo in unison.

"And dinner . . .," yelped Orville, "with no tortillas."

Philo looked at them in mock censure.

"Yaaayy!!" the two voices chorused.

Philo pointed ahead in the gathering dusk to a motel on their right. It wasn't any great shakes as motels go, definitely no Triple A, but it looked clean and comfortable.

Philo pulled into the space next to the office. The three piled out. Philo walked to the back of the truck and opened the door. Clyde rolled out of the camper, throwing his arms around Philo, giving him a sloppy kiss, then followed complacently as the three entered the motel office.

"Room for four," said Philo.

The clerk nodded and handed him a form. "That'll be fifteen dollars," he said.

Philo paid and silently filled out the registration. He handed it to the man, who took it and deposited it into a gray cardboard box.

"Coffee's free," said the man, giving Philo a key.

Philo nodded as Clyde pushed past Echo to drape an arm around his friend.

As the quartet turned and walked out of the office, the clerk spotted Clyde for the first time. His jaw dropped. Clyde, happy to be included, gave a satisfied hoot; then, reaching around Echo, he fondly gave Orville a Sumatran goose.

The Lariat Supper Club: good music and good drinks. New-talent Night. Onstage a girl in a white outfit with sequins from boots to Stetson was singing an old Edy Lynne ballad. She ended her song. The crowd applauded as she stepped off the stage. She walked to the bar.

"Can I leave my guitar here for a while?" she asked.

A big, good-looking guy standing at the bar watched.

"Sure," said the bartender, "let's have her." He reached out and took the guitar.

The good-looking guy caught her eye. He smiled.

She looked at him from beneath half-closed lids. She smiled back.

Sybil's Cafe. It's late. Jukebox and liver smothered. Special of the day. A black-and-white pulled into the parking area. Herb and Putnam stepped out of the car. They walked martially to the cafe, all spit and polish. Inside Sybil was laughing and joking with a table of truckers. The cafe was half full. Herb held the door deferentially for Putnam as they entered. The laughter dropped to a hush as the two officers took a place at the counter. Sybil walked over to them, her face blank and expressionless.

"What'll ya have?" she asked, all business.

"Coffee," said Putnam. He looked at Herb, who nodded the same.

Sybil poured two steaming mugs from the urn and set them in front of the two men. Herb paid.

"Would you know a Philo Beedow?" asked Putnam.

"Beddoe," corrected Herb.

Putnam laid his hat on the counter. "We understand that he hung out around here."

Sybil scratched her head. "Black guy, about five-ten, a hunnerd and eighty?"

"No," Herb interrupted antagonistically. "he ain't black."

"He ain't the one, then," said Sybil. "I don't know him. Will that be all?"

Putnam looked at her. Sybil returned the stare. Putnam dropped his eyes. He took a large gulp of coffee. "Much obliged," he said.

Albuquerque's main street was hopping, but Orville and Echo would never have known it. They sat in the Apache locked in an embrace. Philo pulled over to the curb.

"Why'n't you guys take the truck?" he said. "I want to hear some good music anyway . . . I'll see ya back at the motel."

Orville and Echo untangled themselves as Philo went to get Clyde.

Clyde leaped from the camper with an enthusiastic grunt. Orville poked his head out of the cab. Philo waved him off with a wink, Orville snapped the Apache into gear and moved out. Philo grinned, threw an arm around his hairy companion, and headed down the neon street.

The bars, porn houses, and strip joints beckoned. Bartenders served up beer in frosted schooners, paying scant attention to Clyde. Just another customer. A dirty movie, more beers, a hooker watching and waiting. She tentatively approached Philo and Clyde, then thought better of it. More beers.

Back on the street, Clyde and Philo arm in arm weaved from window to window peering into darkened store fronts. A pet shop. They stopped.

Two puppies romped, ears flopping. A pair of lovebirds cuddled. Two goldfish swam lazily, brushing each other as they passed.

Philo turned, his face thoughtful. The beers were getting to him. He looked back at the pet shop, contemplating great truths. He stuck out his thumb at a passing truck.

The truck pulled up to the motel. Philo waved thanks to the driver, then he and Clyde rolled to the door of their room. Philo fumbled for the key, opened the door, and they both fell in.

Orville and Echo were asleep in each other's arms. Philo looked at them. He nodded gravely as Clyde ambled to the bed and joined the sleeping pair.

Orville woke. He yawned, sat up. "How's it goin'?" he asked groggily.

Philo, definitely three sheets to the wind, rocked uncertainly on the backs of his heels. "Orville, ya gotta get up."

"Why?" asked Orville, still half asleep.

"Cause it ain't right." Philo focused on him with one eye.

"What ain't right?" Orville rubbed the sleep from his eyes.

"What ain't right?" asked Echo, waking. She sat up in the bed.

Philo looked at them profoundly, weaving slightly as he emphasized his words with his hands. "It ain't right that we should have somebody . . . I mean . . . I don't have her yet, ya know . . . but I got somebody . . . and you got somebody . . . even fucking goldfish got somebody!" He dropped his arms.

"Why ain't that right?" Orville was perplexed.

"You don' unnerstan'," mumbled Philo.

"Right," said Echo.

"Yeh, it is." Philo looked at her appreciatively. "That's why we gotta do somethin'."

"We do?" Orville was fully awake now, but highly confused.

"Yup, we gotta." Philo waved one hand around in a circle as if explaining. "Well, come on, come on, get yer clothes on."

"Philo," said Orville, "I don't know what in blazes you're talking about." Shaking his head, he got out of the bed and started to dress.

"Clyde," said Philo drunkenly, "I'm talking 'bout Clyde. My fren'."

The four piled into the Apache, Echo prying her eyes open, Clyde safely ensconced in the rear. Philo turned onto the highway, flicking the radio, loud, singing off key to the music. Turning to Orville and Echo, he interrupted himself.

"You think he don' unnerstan', but he sits back there, and he unnerstan's. He's ve*rrr*y smart."

His companions stared at Philo, bewildered.

"You were right, Orville." Philo continued. "He don' just think about Oreo cookies."

Orville started. "Philo, you don't mean . . ."

"Yup, that's what I mean," slurred Philo with finality.

"Philo . . ." Orville peered at him in concern. "Where ya gonna get Clyde laid in the middle of the night?"

"Well, where ya think?" Philo looked at Orville as though the answer should be obvious. "I ain't gonna get him a hooker. We're goin' ta the zoo!"

Echo and Orville looked at each other in amazement.

Turning several corners, the trio pulled into the confines of the City Park, which housed the zoo and various kiddie rides and exhibits. Strange animal sounds came to them from the enclosures. To Clyde they were not strange at all. The truck shook as he jumped up and down in the camper.

"How the hell do you break into a zoo?" Orville asked the question rhetorically, staring at the dark walls that loomed in front of them.

"It's easy," said Philo. "The whole idea of a zoo is to keep everybody in."

A heavy pounding came from the rear of the truck.

"Ya think he don't know what's happenin'?" Philo jerked his thumb toward the camper. "Ha!" He listened for a moment. Grunts, hoots, and various aboriginal sounds issued from a group of buildings to his left. He drove toward them.

"How do ya know if they got a lady for him?" Orville asked.

"I don' know," said Philo, "but if they do, an' he don' find her, then he pro'ly wouldn't know what to do with her if he did."

Philo braked to a stop beside a high gate. "Hand me that tool kit," he said.

Orville reached under the seat and removed a box of tools. He handed it to Philo.

"What do you want us to do?" asked Echo.

"There just might be somebody guardin' the place. You and Orville wander around on the other side of the zoo 'n' try t' look locked in. We'll be at the monkey house."

Orville and Echo climbed down as Philo opened the rear of the truck. Clyde emerged, sniffing the air, whistling quietly with excitement. Philo removed a coil of rope from the rear and tossed it over his shoulder. Clyde swung to the top of the wall.

"Help me up, Clyde." Philo reached up and grabbed Clyde's dangling arm. The ape pulled Philo up beside him as though he were a child. Philo motioned to Orville in the darkness and reached down to help him. A moment later both men lifted Echo up and over the wall. They jumped down on the other side. Clyde hooted anxiously, pulling at Philo's arm.

"Sheeit," whispered Philo. "He knows where t' go. Go on, I'll whistle twice when I want ya."

Orville and Echo slipped off as two happy primates

headed toward the monkey house. Philo and Clyde walked down the dark path until they came to an open enclosure, an island affair with tree stumps and rocks, surrounded by a deep pit, which separated the viewer from the viewee. A cavelike pile of rocks took up a large part of the island. Behind it, set into the wall, was a small steel door. Clyde moved quickly toward the pit, making sounds Philo had never heard before.

From behind the steel door came answering hoots, and a great thumping of fists on metal.

"Yup," said Philo softly, "there's a lady in there."

He tied one end of the rope firmly to the steel rail that surrounded the pit. The sounds coming from behind the door increased in intensity.

"Shit," mumbled Philo. "Tell ya what, Clyde. Climb on down 'n' see if you can open that thing."

Clyde leaped to the edge of the pit, gazing rapturously at the door from which the sounds were coming. He bounced impatiently, looking at the expanse that separated him from the island. Philo steadied the rope at the edge of the pit and helped Clyde scramble down the concrete wall. Clyde reached the bottom and was onto the island in a flash, making a beeline for the steel door. As Clyde approached, the pounding stopped. Putting his ear to the steel, Clyde listened, making soft noises. All the while, similar soft sounds came from behind the door. He grunted, satisfied, then fumbled with the latch. A couple of mistrials, and then he had the hang of it. He pushed on the latch. Slowly the door swung inward.

If she wasn't the most beautiful orangutan he'd ever seen, you couldn't tell. A sweet simian grin, all teeth and nostrils, crossed Clyde's face. Looking backward over his shoulder, his eyes caught Philo's. Clyde grinned again. Then, with great delicacy, he softly closed the door behind him.

Some hundred yards away, Orville and Echo apprehensively walked the pathways that ran through the zoo. The setting was so natural that, in the darkness, it seemed as if the animals were walking with them. Orville shivered. He heard a sound. He jumped, startled!

"What's that?" he whispered, looking at Echo.

"What's what?"

"I thought I heard something." Orville cocked his head and listened intently. A faint whistle reached his ears. "There! You hear two whistles?"

Echo shook her head.

"Wait." Orville stood still, his finger to his lips.

Echo stepped away from him and peered at a sign fastened to some bars. "Orville, come over here."

"What is it?"

Echo looked at the sign on the cage again. "What's an endangered species?"

"Jesus," Orville looked at her in exasperation. "There, there it is! Two whistles!"

"I didn't hear anything."

A bird, nearby, whistled twice, loud!

Orville grabbed Echo's arm. "Hear it! That's it! Let's go!" He pulled her, stumbling toward the monkey house.

Philo sat waiting by the orang enclosure, his eyes closed, the rope held loosely in his hands, a smile of satisfaction on his face. A wonderful quietness prevailed.

"What is it?" Orville's voice barked in the stillness.

Philo started violently, almost falling into the moat. "What the . . ." He looked around.

"What is it?" Orville repeated.

"You scared the living hell outta me," whispered Philo.

"Well, ya whistled, twice!"

"I didn't whistle. At all."

"Well, goddamnit, somebody whistled."

"Don't matter," said Philo.

"Where's Clyde?" Echo eyed the rope in Philo's hands.

Philo looked across the darkened island. "In heaven, man." Philo smiled. "In heaven."

NINE

A brand-new Jeep pickup, fully equipped with every conceivable extra, drove up to the office of the trailer court. Putnam and Herb, dressed in civilian clothes, hopped out of the rig and marched to the front door. Herb banged on the screen. Several yards away the old pensioner sat sunning himself in a large over-stuffed chair. He was comfortable, shirt off, feet propped up on an orange crate. He looked at the two men banging on the screen with mild curiosity. Finally he cleared his throat. "Hep ya?" he said.

The two officers turned, spotting the scrawny, half-naked body of the old man. They strode over to him. Putnam spoke.

"We're police officers."

Herb nodded his head in agreement, emphasizing the fact.

"We'd like to ask you a few questions," Putnam continued, "about a girl, name of Lynne Halsley-Taylor?"

"Halsey-Taylor," Herb corrected.

The trailer park in Santa Fe, New Mexico, was small but clean, nestled in a grove of trees off the highway. Lynne Halsey-Taylor's trailer sat alone on a concrete pad. The Travellall was gone.

Inside, the trailer stank of old tobacco smoke. Clothes and dirty linen were strewn everywhere. Several TV dinner tins, doubling as ash trays, held bits of food mixed with snuffed butts. A white cardboard box, open, contained two pieces of stale pizza. Crumbs and ashes littered the floor.

·On the bed, on top of the crumpled sheets, Lynne Halsey-Taylor lay asleep, clad in a filmy baby-doll nightie. She moved, throwing a hand over her eyes. One of them was partially swollen. Her cheeks and lips were bruised and discoloured. She moaned in her sleep.

The alarm went off. With a groan, Lynne reached for it, knocking it off the table. The clock shut itself off with a clang as it hit the floor. Lynne groaned again, leaning on one elbow. Groggily she reached for a cigarette. Fumbling with a box of matches, she lit it, her fingers trembled. Pulling herself painfully off the bed, she stumbled to the electric percolator, poured coffee into a dirty cup, then sank back heavily. She sipped at the hot liquid. It burned her mouth. Setting the cup down, she stubbed out the·smoke, reached for a mirror. She looked at herself. She didn't like what she saw. Brushing back her hair, she picked up a makeup brush and dabbed at ·the bruises on her face. She winced. Tentatively she poked at her swollen cheek. She winced again. She studied herself in the mirror, her eyes filling with tears, then, throwing down the brush, she cried.

The Apache moved down the highway at sixty-five, keeping pace with the long freight that charged along the tracks some fifty yards from the road. The locomotive hooted and Philo leaned on the horn. The engineer waved. Echo grinned and handed Philo a peach, taking one for herself. Orville munched on piñon nuts.

Weary of the labour of cracking and extracting the meat, Orville tossed a handful into his mouth and bit down, crunching shells and all. The sound was incredible. Echo and Philo looked at him.

"Orville . . .?" said Philo.

"Hmmmm," replied Orville, continuing to stuff nuts into his maw, cracking and crunching with gusto.

"Nothin'," said Philo. He turned up the volume on the radio.

A sign on the shoulder of the highway flashed by: SANTA FE, EIGHTEEN MILES. Orville continued cracking and crunching.

"Orville!" Echo looked at him, hard.

"Hmm?"

"That's drivin' me crazy."

"What is?" asked Orville, stuffing another handful of nuts into his mouth.

"The way you're eatin' them things." Echo wrinkled her nose.

"Oh . . . sorry." He opened the window and blew them out.

"Thanks," said Echo.

"S'awright." Orville beamed at her. He reached into the bag behind them and pulled out an apple. The road was clear, the air clean, the desert had a refreshing smell of sage. The sky was blue. Orville crashed into the apple. The piñons sounded better. Echo and Philo looked at him again. Sheepishly he met their eyes, sighed wearily, rolled down the window, and heaved the apple after the receding freight.

The Black Widows were out in force. Nine bikes roared down the freeway toward Newhall, half of them carrying two riders, mute testimony to a penchant for losing machines. They poured off the freeway, single file onto the frontage road, then regrouped. Cholla at their head, a formidable block of chrome and steel, they rolled down the highway, pulling into Sybil's Cafe crackling and rumbling, churning up clouds of dust. A half-dozen semis were parked around the small building. The bikers reined up. Parking their mounts in clusters of three and six, with Cholla in the lead, they moved, a solid mass, into the cafe.

Lunch hour the cafe was crowded. The bikers fell in

looking for a spot to park their asses. They flung themselves around with ritualized unconcern stomping through everyone's space. Sybil, working the tables and the counter, ignored them with a studied indifference.

"Say hey, little lady," said Dallas, finally catching Sybil's eye, "what's good to eat?"

Sybil looked at him as if he were a roach in the stew. "It's all good," she said. She walked past him and rounded the counter, calling out two orders to the chef. She picked up three steaming plates and moved back into the crowded room.

"Don't you got a special of the day?" Elmo drawled as she walked by.

"Liver and onions," said Sybil. "Why'n't you read the menu?"

Elmo bristled. "I'd rather talk to you. Philo Beddoe around?"

Sybil regarded him narrowly, her eyes squinting in distaste. "You want to talk, take a walk. You want to eat, take a seat." She turned away and delivered the plates as the cafe broke up with laughter.

Frank, incensed at the truckers' amusement, strode to the counter. He glared at Lester, a solidly build road jockey who was enjoying Elmo's discomfort. "What's so funny, lardass?"

The trucker, his mouth full of French fries, looked up disdainfully. "Tell you what," he said slowly. "You turn 'roun' and walk outta here, and I'll forget you said that and won't tell nobody 'at you drink horsepiss."

The other truckers roared as Frank flushed at the affront.

Sybil, seeing it all line up, walked over and removed Lester's plate. "I'll keep this warm for ya, Lester," she called out. "You want that last piece of lemon meringue?"

"Yeah, this won't take but a minute." He turned to Frank. "Let's go, cunt!"

Frank, livid at having been put down, could hardly wait. Lester stood up and started for the door, Frank hot behind him. The whole cafe followed.

Then, with no warning, Frank aimed a vicious kick. It caught the trucker in the small of the back, knocking him through the door. Charging after the man, Frank caught him with a heavy right to the jaw. Lester backed off, shaking his head to clear it as Frank charged again. This time the biker was met by a pile-driving left followed with a hard right that caught Frank behind the ear, staggering him. The spectators cheered. Catching his breath, Frank turned and locked his arm around Lester's neck. With his free fist, Frank bashed the trucker in the face. Frank screamed as Lester's elbow caught him full in the balls. The blood drained from his face. Lester backhanded the biker and followed up with a right and a left that sent Frank flying. Two blows to the gut and one to the ear brought him to his knees.

Dallas, unable to bear the sight of a Widow losing, lunged at Lester. Without missing a beat, Lester met him with an uppercut that rattled his horns. A rain of blows drove the biker up against the wall of the cafe. He was no match for the now thoroughly riled trucker. Lester pummelled him mercilessly. Three more Widows, sensing Dallas's fate, attacked. They were met by a wall of truckers. Seconds later the parking lot erupted in a free-for-all as more Widows charged. The truckers evened the odds, wading into the ranks of the bikers. Fists flew. Bodies bounced and slid as bone found flesh and heads cracked. Conspicuously absent from the donny-brook was Cholla, who, safe with Sybil, watched from inside the cafe.

As the battle stormed, a semi rolled into the lot. The driver and his companion surveyed the carnage.

"Shit, Bobby," said the driver, "looks like we almost got here too late."

Bobby, riding shotgun, pulled out his bridgework and smiled. "Jest leave us a little bit now, boys. Goddammit, hurry up, Leon!"

The rig approached the parking area. Leon spotted the cluster of three bikes and grinned. "I'm gonna save a few of 'em for us. Hold on!" He pointed the semi toward the motorcycles, tromped the accelerator, and let out three blasts on the air horns. Fighters scattered as the semi barrelled through the parking area. Elmo, having just been heaved over a pickup, got up, spitting asphalt.

He watched in horror as the semi bore down on the choppers. "Oh no!" he screamed.

A fist from nowhere spared him the agony. The truck crunched into the three gleaming machines. Two bikes flew skyward. The third bike was dragged a hundred feet before disappearing beneath eighteen massive wheels. It emerged an unrecognizable chunk of bent and twisted metal.

The shock of seeing their bikes destroyed was too much for the Widows. As a man, the dozen bikers raced for the surviving machines and kicked them into life. Packing double, they roared onto the highway, Cholla, shaking his head, a stunned general in full retreat.

You've got to have a feel for the kind of bar to go to, to find fighters. Orville was seldom wrong. Still, Santa Fe was a strange city. He sat at the counter slowly downing a cold one. The place was quiet, no action. A couple of bored cowboys in grubby denims and worn boots, somebody's grandmother, a well-oiled Indian asleep in a corner booth. Orville finished his beer and motioned to the bartender. Leaning over the bar, Orville questioned him. The bartender looked puzzled, thought for a moment, then shook his head. Orville nodded and paid for the beer. He stepped outside in the hot sunlight.

Another bar, livelier, terrible music from the Wurlitzer. Conversation but no action. Disgusted, Orville headed for the door, pausing only to drop a quarter into the box. Three good country-western tunes. Enriching the culture of New Mexico.

A third bar, funky, dirty, a real Mexican *cantina*. Noisy, a hint of excitement in the air. A different breed. The bartender earned his pay. Bottles, glasses, and pitchers moved across the bar in a steady stream. At the pool table that dominated the room, a huge black man sank balls methodically. This time, Orville was listening. Heads nodded, earnest faces, gestures. Glances. The black man occasionally looked up from the table, aloof, strong, sullen. Orville shook hands, checked his watch, and started out. The black man blocked his way. Orville backpedalled to the door. It takes all kinds.

Orville climbed into the Apache. Across the street they were setting up a tent and stacking chairs. A large sign said REVIVAL TONIGHT! Orville gunned it past the tent. The P.A. system played a whole 'nother kind of music. Orville hummed to himself happily. Ten minutes later he turned into the motel.

The room, while not the Best Western, was clean and comfortable. Philo was sprawled on a chair. Clyde hunkered down asleep in a corner. Orville's look told it all.

"They know me?" asked Philo. He sat up in the chair feeling the twinge of excitement that preceded action.

"Nope," said Orville, "even money." His grin reached from ear to ear.

Philo relaxed, satisfied. "Anything else?"

Orville cracked himself a beer from the six pack on the table and took a swig. "Yeh, black guy, name's Kincaid, the local champ." He eyed Philo. "Taller'n you, pro'ly weighin' around two-forty. I asked around . . ."

"Yeah?" Philo's eyes were hard.

"They say he stacks up to Tank Murdoch."

Philo nodded. "Tank Murdoch, huh?"

Orville smiled. "Just like 'em all, Tank's gonna fall. Oh one other thing."

Philo looked up.

Orville tipped the beer to his lips. "He fights dirty!"

"I don't know why you won't let me watch," pouted Echo. She sat unhappily between Philo and Orville as the Apache moved through the outskirts of Santa Fe. The late-afternoon sun beat through the windshield. The road shimmered in the heat.

Orville took a pull from his beer and looked at Echo. "Lotta guys," he said thoughtfully, "don't like women around for such goin's-on. Makes 'em feel self-conscious. B'sides, it could get messy."

Echo shook her head. "My daddy taught me t' take care of myself."

"Well, that's how it's gotta be," said Orville with finality.

Echo sat aloof, unaccepting. She looked out the window. Philo felt her distress. "Shit, Orville," he said at last. "Won't harm nothin'. Echo, you just keep outta sight."

Echo smiled, happy in her victory. Orville shrugged.

The Apache rolled on, past the switching yards and into an area of light industry. An occasional cracker-box house sat desolate between rows of warehouses. Orville, consulting a small scrap of paper, issued directions.

"Stockyards should be comin' up pretty soon," he said.

The Apache bore down past acres of corrals and sorting pens. The stench was unbelievable.

"Whoeee," said Echo, wrinkling her nose. "I sure don't care for the perfume they're wearin'."

Philo slowed the truck as they passed a processing plant.

"It's on past the slaughterhouse," said Orville, pointing to a large building into which funnelled a dozen ramps from the sorting pens. "Keep your eyes peeled for the cold room."

"What's it look like?" asked Echo.

"Like it's behind the loading dock," said Orville.

Philo turned down a narrow lane, skirting the pens, and rolled to a stop by the loading dock. The cold room sat to one side. A man stood in front of the building. He checked his watch as the Apache pulled in.

"You Orville Boggs?" the man asked.

"You got it," said Orville. The trio stepped down from the cab.

The man nodded and pulled open a large overhead door.

He motioned them in and closed the door behind him.

The cold room was filled with sides of beef, the carcasses hanging in neat rows from hooks attached to ceiling trolleys. The smell of ripe meat permeated the air. An area in the centre of the cold room was cleared of hanging flesh, forming a small arena.

Echo, unobtrusively, disappeared into the hanging beef behind the crowd that had gathered.

Kincaid placidly observed Philo, his arms folded across his chest. The men standing beside him appraised Philo openly. They whispered, smiling and shaking their heads disparagingly, noting the difference in the size of the two fighters. Hands reached into pockets for money. Kincaid's man drifted through the crowd collecting the bills. When he was through, he walked over to Orville.

"How much you want?" he asked, licking his lips.

"How much you got?" Orville's face remained blank.

"Twelve hundred," replied the man. He wanted all he could get.

Orville nodded. "We'll take it."

The man smiled and relaxed. "Ya got to show me somethin' besides conversation."

Orville pulled out his wallet and removed twelve one-hundred-dollar bills. His eyes searched the ceiling. It was a lot of money, damn near every cent they had.

"I'll hold it," said the man. He reached for the money.

Orville looked at Philo, his eyebrow raised questioningly. Philo measured the man with his eyes. He nodded.

"You want to show me yours?" asked Orville.

The man fanned out a roll. It was enough. "Where do you want us to send the body?" the man asked.

"Why'n't ya save yer breath?" said Orville, moving back to Philo. "It's enough yer gonna lose yer money."

The man gave Orville a quick dirty look and walked back to his fighter. He talked briefly with the black man. Kincaid nodded, balling his gigantic hands into fists. He slowly removed his outer shirt. Philo watched from across the way.

Kincaid was built like the right half of the Rams' line. His biceps bulged in the cold. He looked solid granite.

The crowd was getting impatient. Several voices called out to get it on. They felt the cold too. Philo removed his shirt.

"Philo, you ready?" Orville stepped back into the ranks of hanging beef.

Philo nodded. The two combatants stared at each other, then moved into the centre of the arena. They circled each other warily, looking for an opening.

The black man lunged, aiming a sledgehammer blow at Philo's head. Philo backstepped and ducked as the huge fist cut past his left ear. Another lunge by Kincaid caught Philo off balance. The blow glanced off his shoulder. The black man dropped his guard and caught two quick ones to the face. He jerked back, brushing a sweating brown hand across his cheek. The crowd roared at the first blows. Kincaid bored in, crushing Philo to him. He ground his chin into Philo's ear, then cuffed him repeatedly in the kidneys before Philo could break away. Philo shoved the black man away with both hands, then landed a hard right to his belly. Kincaid grunted. Bouncing off a side of beef, he landed a heavy left to Philo's cheek. Philo backed away. As the black man followed up, Philo feinted, then caught him with two quick jabs to the head. Kincaid's arms flew up to protect his face. Philo bore in wth a combination to the black man's midsection, driving him back into the circle of onlookers. Kincaid grunted, grabbing at his gut. As Philo pushed in, Kincaid aimed a terrific kick to the groin. As his leg came up, Philo turned, catching the blow on his thigh. He retaliated with a right that split the man's ear. Blood splattered the big man's neck. Reaching up, Kincaid grabbed a hook hanging from the overhead trolley. He pulled it off and faced Philo in a crouch, the hook swinging in his hand. He lashed out. The sharp steel whistled past Philo's gut. The black man grinned as Philo bounced out of reach. Kincaid lashed out again, narrowly missing Philo's head. As the hook whizzed past, Philo sidestepped, catching the black man's arm. He twisted. Kincaid groaned as the hook clattered to the ground. Philo kicked it away. Kincaid cursed and wrenched his arm loose. He backed off slowly, his eyes narrowing. Philo circled, watching the black man's hands. Both men were breathing heavily.

Kincaid moved quickly. He jumped and grabbed the overhead trolley tracks, launching himself and landing with both feet square into Philo's chest. Philo went down. The black man threw himself on top of him. They rolled on the floor, Kincaid grabbing at Philo's head, searching for his eyes. Philo bit down. Hard. The black man screamed as Philo's teeth met in the flesh of his forearm. He leaped to his feet, nursing the injured arm. Philo followed, unleashing a right, a left, then another right to the black man's jaw. Kincaid fell back, stunned, gasping. The black staggered and fell against one side of beef, and then another, stumbling to get away from the pounding fists. He kicked out at the blurred form pursuing him. The ceiling spun as Philo's fists battered him. He grabbed at a carcass to steady himself. A right uppercut tore him loose, and a left hook sent him reeling across the concrete. Philo was relentless. A smash to the nose contorted Kincaid with pain. Another blow. Laser whiteness. Then an explosion of sound, erupting into silence, fading with the light into blackness.

Philo looked around. Breathing deeply, the man at his feet was motionless. Philo heard the silence. He didn't feel the cold. The crowd stared at him and at the unconscious Kincaid. Orville handed Philo his shirt. Slowly he put it on.

A sigh filled the room. Then gave way to a hushed babble of disjointed phrases and muttered curses. Orville crossed to the man holding the money. They faced each other, a side of beef hanging between them. Stamped on the carcass, under the USDA shield, was a bright purple circle reading CHOICE.

"I'll thank you for our money now," said Orville. He held out his hand.

The man looked at him narrowly, the hint of a smirk on his face. "What money?"

Orville, taken aback, leaned forward. "Now wait a minute."

The man smiled as the crowd of bettors grew silent. "You're not about to tell all of these boys that you're gonna take their money, now are ya?" He looked around at the partisan faces. Several people laughed.

Across the room Philo finished pulling on his shirt. He tucked it in and looked toward Orville and the man. Something was wrong. Orville's face was flushed, angry. Philo took one step toward them.

A shot exploded in the cold room, reverberating off the frosty walls. With a solid thunk, a bullet embedded itself deep in the side of beef between Orville and the man holding the money. The hole, dead centre in the purple circle, was six inches above the man's head. The man stared at it, his eyes widening. All voices stopped as another shot rang out. With a thwack of bullet meeting flesh, a second hole appeared, a quarter of an inch from the first one.

"That was so's nobody thinks the first one was an acccident." Echo's voice rang clear and cold in the chilly air.

She was standing beside a meat dolly, her pistol held in front of her with both hands. All eyes turned. Echo shifted the barrel slightly, until it was aimed directly at the forehead of Kincaid's man. He looked straight down the barrel.

Orville smiled. He held out his hand again. "I think you owe us some money," he said.

The Apache pushed through the dusk to the strains of funky blue grass as the lights of Santa Fe receded.

"Did you see this little filly shoot?" Orville couldn't contain his pride or surprise. "She could pick a gnat off the ass of a water buffalo."

Philo laughed. "Orville, you never seen a water buffalo."

"Don't matter," said Orville. He leaned over and gave

Echo a kiss. "I've seen a gnat."

Philo regarded Echo for a moment. She sat primly between the two men, a look of quiet satisfaction on her face. "Where'd you learn to shoot like that?" he asked.

Echo, pleased at the attention and feeling good, smiled. "I told you my daddy taught me t'take care of m'self."

Orville gave her another kiss and hugged her. "Well," he said, "you took good care of us, too, m' darlin'."

"Kiss her one for me, too," grinned Philo.

"Do it yerself," said Orville, "See what you been missin'."

Philo looked at his partner, then, with a huge smile, reached over and grabbed Echo, planting his lips on hers. The truck swerved to one side of the road, then the other.

"Jesus Christ," yelled Orville, grabbing the wheel. "I said kiss her, not kill us." Reaching across them, he aimed the Apache down the highway while Philo hugged and kissed away. The grin on Orville's mug was as fine as the fiddle that danced happily from the speakers.

The old pensioner was asleep in a ratty aluminum chair. From his hand dangled a hose. Water spurted from the nozzle, inundating and drowning a struggling bed of pansies. The old man snored, oblivious, as six motorcycles roared down the drive of the trailer court, pulling to a stop before him. Twelve Black Widows looked at the old man, then back at each other.

"How come he ain't movin'?" whispered Frank, his bruises very much in evidence.

"Ya think he's dead?" Elmo peered intently at the pensioner.

"Maybe we oughta split," suggested Bruno, another Widow, apprehensively looking for signs of life and seeing none.

"Shit, man," said Elmo, starting to get off, "if he's the only one here . . . let's . . ."

"Sit your ass on that bike!" barked Cholla. He raised his quirt warningly. Elmo sat down slowly. "But it's only one old man."

Cholla looked at Elmo menacingly, then precisely tapped the tank of his bike as though talking to a schoolchild. "One old lady just kicked shit outta all of us 'n' nearly blew your balls off. All we want here is information. The first one who fucks it up deals with me." His eyes touched each Widow.

Elmo shrugged his shoulders.

Getting off his bike Cholla walked to the old man, carefully avoiding the spray of water. He leaned over the aluminum chair. "Excuse me, mister."

There was no response. The old man's mouth hung open. From its cavernous interior came only a faint wheezing.

"Hey, you in there?" Cholla grabbed the old man's shoulder and shook it.

With a snort the old man woke up, a trickle of spittle oozing down his chin. "Huh? Wha . . ." He jerked upright, looking around in confusion. "What is it? Who're you?"

Cholla stepped back as the spray from the nozzle moved aimlessly. "I'm lookin'," he moved again as the water erratically followed him, "for a lady used to stay here. She went with a guy named Philo Beddoe."

"Don't know no Philo Beddoe," grumbled the pensioner, irked at having been awakened.

"Girl's name was Halsey-Taylor. Lynne Halsey-Taylor," continued Cholla.

The old man thought for a moment. "Yep. She was here, but the guy was named Schyler. Couldn't play cribbage worth a rat's pecker."

Cholla twirled the riding crop in his hands. "You sure?"

"Course I'm sure," replied the old man. He glared at Cholla as though he were a mental defective. "Been playing cribbage for forty-seven years." He shook his head.

"I mean about the girl," said Cholla, irritated but holding himself in check.

"Gotta be one jim-dandy of a girl," continued the old man. "You're the third one come ask about her since she left for Denver."

120

Cholla's eyes narrowed to tiny slits. He tapped the quirt against his palm, nodding his head reflectively. "Ya don't say." Turning, he looked down at his boots. His face turned several shades of purple. Both boots were full of water.

It was late afternoon, almost dusk. Putnam's Jeep was parked off the road in a shallow depression. Several yards away from the vehicle Putnam and Herb blasted away at a variety of bottles and cans, their faces studied in earnest concentration. Roving ambassadors for the National Rifle Association, the John Birch Society, and perhaps, stretching the point for Herb's benefit, the Ku Klux Klan. The bottles and cans remained upright and intact, mute testimony to their marksmanship.

Putnam grimaced as he pulled off a shot, missing the entire row. He would have preferred a moving target. Definitely more fun. He kept his eye peeled hopefully for anything that ran, flew, or crawled. He squeezed the trigger again, finally sending a rusted beer can flying. He yelled in triumph!

Herb fanned two quick ones at the bouncing can. To his astonishment, both connected, tearing the can in half. With arrogant indifference, Herb brought the barrel to his lips and blew away the trailing wisps of smoke. Putnam stared, incredulous, pissed, knowing he would have to live with this.

The radio in the Jeep was tuned to the New Mexico police frequency, which now crackled, indicating a message to follow. After a moment, the nasal voice of the dispatcher oozed through the speakers.

"Car one-oh-three. Car one-oh-three, proceed to the intersection of Interstate 40 and Velásquez Road for a six-oh-two."

Car 103 answered perfunctorily. "Gotcha. Over."

Still smoldering and petulant, Putnam commented. "Eight to five, their six-oh-two is the same as our four-oh-six."

"No way," contradicted Herb. "It's got to be the same as

121

our three-oh-nine or at most our two-one-three."

"You're crazy," Putnam disagreed. "No New Mexican six-oh-two can come close to a California three-oh-nine."

"When's the last time you went out on a three-oh-nine?" asked Herb.

"Maybe three or four months," replied Putnam. "But that don't mean that I don't know our three-oh-nine ain't more than their damn six-oh-two."

Herb nodded his head. "What time you got?" he asked.

Putnam consulted his watch. "Six-oh-seven," he said.

The radio crackled to life. "Unit one-oh-three. Abort that six-oh-two, one-oh-three. Proceed to Velasquez Road and Interstate 40 for a six-oh-seven."

Putnam and Herb stared at each other. It was going to be a long night.

The night was clear, a touch of chill in the air. The stars were incredible. A full moon outlined the rolling hills as the pungent smell of sage filled the air. Philo looked into the distance, taking it all in.

The moon climbed higher, bathing the campsite in a gentle light. Philo sat by the fire staring into the flames. He poured himself a cup of coffee and leaned back against his roll. He sipped the hot liquid slowly, warming his hands on the cup. Orville snored as the fire popped and crackled.

"You know," said Philo, "a lot of people would think I'm crazy, goin' off across the country to find a girl I only met. But she's not jus' any girl." He took another gulp and tossed a piece of wood on the fire. It caught and blazed. He smiled to himself and looked over at Orville. "I'm not like Orville when it comes to that," he continued. "It take me a long time to get to know a girl and even longer to let her get to know me. Do you know what I mean?" He kicked at the ground. "You know I'm not scared a' no man, but when it comes to sharin' my feelings with a girl, my stomach turns to Royal Gelatin." He gazed at the moon, then turned his attention back to the coffee. "Don't suppose that ever

122

happens to you, huh?"

A coyote howled in the distance, a long, mournful wail. A moment later an answering howl, fainter, cut through the night air.

"I guess that's what it's all about," said Philo. "We go on howlin' till we find somebody who'll howl back." He turned back to the fire. "Aw what the shit . . . let's turn in."

Orville let out a snort in his sleep. Echo's arm reached out from their bedroll and wrapped around Orville and hugged him close to her.

Clyde draped a hairy arm lovingly around Philo's neck. Philo looked at him. It was nice to have someone to talk to.

The crash of pins and the distinctive sound of sixteen-pound balls echoing down polished alleys mixed with the din of conversation and the clink of beer bottles.

Lynne Halsey-Taylor bent over her ball, sighting down the alley. She concentrated deeply and muttered to herself. "If thi is a strike, that means Loretta Lynn, you can move over. A strike carries Halsey-Taylor to the top."

As she finished her magic incantation, she moved toward the line and let fly. The ball carried true, swerving only at the last second, crashing into the pins to leave one standing. Lynne shook her head, waiting for the ball to come back. She picked it up from the return and faced the pins again. She held the ball cradled in her left hand and squinted down the alley. "That's all right," she mumbled, "that just means that it's gonna take a might longer. But we don't give up. If I wipe you out, ol' pin, that means next year at this time it's Halsey-Taylor in the Grand Ol' Opry!"

She let fly again. This time the spell worked. The ball rolled down the alley without wavering and picked off the one pin. Lynne smiled and reached for the bottle of beer sitting by the score table. She took a swig as the automatic pin setters did their job. The ball rolled back, and she turned to it.

"This one is for a top-ten record, *Cashbox*, *Billboard*,

and *Record World*." Lynne dried her hands on a towel and reached for the ball. She concentrated, aimed, and let the ball slide smoothly off her fingers.

"Top ten, with a bullet!"

The ball slid just to the left of the head pin, then cut to the right. The pins exploded; a STRIKE!

"Allll rrrriiiiigggggghhhht!"

Lynne turned, took another pull from her bottle, and marked her score.

A tall, wide, and handsome fella, who by the looks of him had to be named Jimmie Lee or Billy Joe, or maybe Joe Don, walked up behind her. He watched her bowl the next ball. Eight pins went down. He leaned over and checked the label on Lynne's bottle. He motioned for the waitress, ordered two Coors, then watched as Lynne went for the spare. She saw him. As she turned back to the alley, she smiled.

"And this one," she mouthed, "is for a great, big, big . . ." She started her move, ". . . beautiful . . ."

She let the ball go. It felt good. She didn't have to wait for the pins to go down. She turned into a wide, white smile and the man behind it.

"Mighty fine pickup," he said. He held out a beer.

Lynne Halsey-Taylor smiled back. She wouldn't have to wait a year for this fantasy.

Just outside Taos, New Mexico. Breakfast was over, the campsite neat and tidy. Sun beginning to dry the dew. A time to relax for a spell. Philo, dressed in a sweat suit with a towel draped around his neck, dumped the dregs of his second cup of coffee. He called to Orville.

"Hey, Orville. You mind handlin' things tonight? I'm feelin' restless."

Orville walked over to him. "That all?"

"Yeah, just want to get off by myself."

"Sure," said Orville, "Don't worry 'bout nothin'."

Philo waved at Echo and stopped by the camper. He reached in and scratched Clyde's head. A hairy arm probed his shirt. "See ya later, ol' buddy." Philo turned and trotted out of the campground onto the highway.

When he reached the blacktop he broke into a lope, moving easily down the roadway. Philo maintained the pace for a couple of miles, then opened up, pushing himself for several hundred yards until the thin mountain air seared his lungs. He slowed, taking several deep breaths. His heart was pounding. Taking off again he paced himself, falling into a steady rhythm he could maintain without tiring. A car whizzed past. Philo turned and began walking backward. Another car approached. He raised his thumb. It roared by. A cluster of pillion nuts hanging from a tree caught his eye. He pulled some off and cracked one in his teeth. Bitter. He spat out the nut and tossed the cluster away. Sometimes he couldn't understand Orville's eating habits. A large vehicle approached.

Inside the Travelall, Lynn Halsey-Taylor smiled at herself in the mirror. Looking ahead at the large figure walking by the side of the road, she touched the back of her hair and slowed as she approached the hitchhiker. He was tall, about 6 feet 4 inches, 220 pounds. She was just about even with him.

"Jesus H. Christ!" Lynne floored the Travelall. It was Philo!

As she accelerated, Philo recognized her. He waved his arms and yelled. "Hey!! HEY!! LYNNE, IT'S ME!!" He started running after the truck.

Lynne watched him in the rear-view mirror. "Damn!" she said, slowing to a halt as Philo, breathing hard, ran up. He rested his hand on the window and smiled up at her.

He caught his breath. "Fancy meetin' you here," he said.

Lynne looked at him. She shook her head. "Fancy, hell. Incredible is more like it! What are you doin' here?"

Philo opened the door and climbed in. "Followin' you."

The Travellall moved down the road toward Taos, Philo bringing her to date.

"So," he said, "I knew somethin' had to be the matter,

you just takin' off like that and all. So I thought I'd better follow you and find out."

Lynne's face softened. "You thought you better, huh?" She shook her head again.

"Yeah," his face was one big grin. "You never even got to meet Clyde."

Much later later Philo and Lynne lay together; the moon silhouetted the pines framed in the motel window. Their fingers touched. How gentle Philo was. Lynne was aware how violent this strange man could be. His unexpected tenderness touched and surprised her. She leaned over and kissed him. Philo lightly combed her hair with his fingertips, then moved his hand down her breasts, along the softness of her skin. She trembled as his fingers found a special spot. He pulled her to him. They kissed gently. Her hair brushed against his face. Philo ran his fingers down her back, touching the dimples where the nerve endings ran close to the skin. She moved against him. He nuzzled her, animal-like. She responded, gently biting his chest, tasting the saltiness of his body. Their hands explored each other. She could feel his urgency. Lynne leaned back, holding his face in her hands, her eyes mirroring her delight. "Let me look at you," she said.

Philo smiled, turning to her.

She moved on top of him. "What are you smiling at?" Her body moved with his.

His eyes twinkled. "You askin' why I followed."

The Travellall sped east, moving toward the campground. The headlights caught and mesmerised a jackrabbit, freezing it into immobility by the side of the road. Lynne was at the wheel, Philo beside her, leaning back against the seat. The radio played softly.

Lynne chewed her lower lip thoughtfully. "I know where he's keeping the money now," she said. "I just have to wait for the right moment to get it."

"My way would be quicker," said Philo. He squinted into

126

the darkness.

Lynne frowned. Her hands tightened on the wheel. "Philo, you promised." She pressed on the accelerator. "Now don't make me sorry I told you. Don't make me afraid to believe you."

Philo leaned over and kissed her on the neck. "I won't ever make you sorry," he said.

"We almost there?" she asked.

Philo sat back in the seat. "Just down the road a piece," he said. "Just past that scrub oak."

Lynne slowed to a stop by the side of the road. Through the trees the light of a campfire flickered.

"Can you come on down and meet ever'-body?" Philo asked.

Lynne hesitated. "I better be gettin' back." She smiled. "Let's do it when we have more time."

Philo nodded. "You're right," he said. "See ya tomorrow." He slid over and kissed her. He held her for a moment, then climbed out.

She stopped him. "Philo . . ."

He waited.

Lynne searched his face, started to say something, then changed her mind. "You're somthin' else again." She put the Travelall into gear. Philo waved as she made a U turn and drove off into the night.

Walking through the pines, Philo reached the campsite. Orville and Echo were asleep, curled up in the bedroll. He stopped to look at them for a second, then made his way to the camper. Clyde was overjoyed. Finally free and with Philo, he leaped for the lower branches of an oak and swung joyfully. Arm over arm, he climbed upward. Philo followed him. Together they cavorted happily in the darkness.

TEN

Five people stood in earnest conversation beside the orangutan enclosure at the Albùquerque Zoo. Putnam and Herb, dressed for the road, were talking animatedly with two plain-clothesmen, while the curator of the zoo stood to one side, wringing his hands in anxiety.

"We heard your police call on our radio," said Putnam, "and it seemed like more than just a coincidence."

"We appreciate your interest," said one of the cops. He wrote something in the small black notebook he carried.

The curator stepped forward, almost timidly. "Nothing like this has ever happened before," he interjected. "We don't know what to make of it." He looked at the four men standing around him.

"How did you first discover your ape was raped?" asked the second cop formally. It was business as usual.

"Well," sighed the curator, "we discovered it this morning when she was supposed to mate with Eric, the orang we got from the St. Louis Zoo." The curator's hands fluttered. "In exchange, we let them mate two of our giraffes and a wildebeast." He looked at the ground, then nervously into the faces of the four men.

"I don't understand," said Herb.

"Well," the curator turned to Herb, "zoos around the

country have a mutual service . . ."

"No," interrupted Herb, "about the . . . uh, rape." He stepped back a pace. The man's twitching made him nervous.

"Well," said the curator again, "this morning when we put Eric in Zelda's cage, she nearly tore him apart." He shuffled his feet, embarrassed. "Orangs are a lot like people, and we knew that day before yesterday she was hotter'n a pistol. So it didn't make sense." He paused.

"So?" said Putnam impatiently.

"So we examined her after she stopped beating on poor Eric." The curator pointed to an ape sitting despondently in a cage next to the enclosure.

"And . . . and . . .," urged Putnam.

The curator looked at Putnam with distaste. "And we found that she had already engaged in . . . she'd already had . . ."

"I got the picture," said Putnam.

The curator continued. "Now, there is no way any of our apes could have done it. I personally have been locking them all in for the night." He emphasized his words with a pointed finger. "Somebody, I mean some orang, had to come in from the outside and open the outside door."

The first cop turned to his partner, notebook at the ready. "Should we take prints?" he asked.

"Shut up," said the second cop. He turned to Putnam. "Does the guy you're chasing have an ape that she would go for?"

"I don't know," replied Putnam. "I've never seen him. Don't they all look alike?"

The curator stepped between the two men. "It would have to be another orangutan, of course. And as a matter of fact, they don't *all* look alike at all. Take Spencer over there, for example." He indicated another orangutan sitting in a cage. "He's much more humanoid in appear . . ."

Putnam interrupted the curator impatiently. "Who gives a damn," he said. "I'm looking for a fugitive, not a single club for baboons."

The curator, miffed, regarded Putnam sourly. He drew himself up to his full height. "These are not baboons," he said condescendingly. "Although baboons *are* members of the Dryopithecines, they would never mate with an orang . . ."

"Will you shut up!" said the second cop.

The curator twitched, shocked at such a blatant display of bad manners.

"Now, the way I see it," the second cop continued, "some ape broke in and raped your Zelda. Right?"

The curator pointedly ignored him.

"RIGHT?" The policeman glared.

Reluctantly the curator answered, his feelings hurt. "Yes," he said, "that's right."

"And," continued the second cop, "after breaking and entering, you say that your tests say *she was raped*. Right?"

"That's correct," said the curator.

"Yet when you brought her Eric, she didn't dig him at all. Right?"

The curator nodded. "Yes."

"So it's possible," said the policeman—he looked accusingly at the curator—"that she wasn't raped at all, but was a consenting . . ."

"Jesus Christ!" exploded Putnam, staring at the cop.

The cop bristled. He pointed a finger at Putnam. "Look," he said, "I don't know how you guys conduct an investigation in California, but if you don't like what we do here, then fuck off!"

"I would appreciate," said the curator haughtily, "your not using such language around the Pongo Pygmaeus. They're very sensitive and . . ." He stopped. All four policemen had something to say about the Pongo Pygmaeus.

The Apache pulled into the campsite. Philo braked sharply and cut the ignition, bringing the truck to a halt a few feet from Orville and Echo. They were both still asleep, wrapped in the bedroll. A pot of coffee bubbled softly on the still-smoldering campfire. Philo jumped out of the truck humming, still high from the night before, anticipating a beautiful day. He walked to the back of the camper and opened the door. Clyde bounced out, carrying a string of gorgeous rainbows. He ambled over to Orville and dropped the fish with a splat next to his nose. Clyde hunkered back expectantly, holding onto the end of the string.

"Jesus Christ!" Orville jerked awake like a spastic marionette.

Clyde pulled the string of fish up and down in front of Orville like a Yo-Yo, hooting with pleasure.

Orville blinked, staring at the bouncing fish. "Gawd damn," he said. "I don't believe what I'm seein'. I must be still asleep and dreamin'."

Philo squatted down next to him. "Get your lazy butt outta bed," he said. "You ain't dreamin'."

Orville rubbed his face, keeping a wary eye out for the fish. "Sure had a weird one last night."

"Yeah?" Philo cocked an eyebrow.

"Yeah," Orville scratched his head. "I dreamed some crazy sonofabitch was singin' 'n' swingin' through the trees like Tarzan a' the apes, with an ape! The only thing missin' was some native drums and I'd a' swore I was in Africa."

Philo grinned and picked up one of Orville's boots. He pegged it, hitting the sleeping Echo in the ass. She woke up with a start.

"Hey!" she sat up suddenly. "Whyd'ja do that?"

"I think," yawned Orville, "he's tryin' ta tell us somethin'!"

"What's that?" Echo stretched, then rubbed the sleep from her eyes.

"What you so all-fired happy about, Philo?" Orville studies his friend. "I never see you this way less'n . . ."

Philo looked at Orville with a self-satisfied smile.

". . . ya got laid!" A look of delight crossed Orville's face.

"You just hitched on down the road and got yourself laid, didn't ya?"

"That ain't all," said Philo.

Echo crawled out of the sack, brushing the hair out of her eyes. She poured coffee and brought Philo a cup as Orville tumbled out of the roll and slipped on his pants.

"Don't tell me Clyde got laid again, too?" He buttoned up his shirt.

Philo smiled. "I found Lynne Halsey-Taylor."

There was a moment of silence as the news sunk in. Both Echo and Orville looked at Philo dumbfounded.

"How'd ya do that?" asked Echo, finally.

"You'll never believe it. She drove right by me when I was hitchin'."

"Well, where is she?" demanded Orville.

Philo shrugged. "She's got some stuff to straighten out today. She's gonna sing at a place in Taos tonight. We'll meet her later."

"Well, goddamn!" Orville slapped his thigh, pleased. "That sure is good news. Means we'll be goin' home soon, huh?"

"Don't see why not," grunted Philo.

Orville pulled on his boots. "Well," he said, "while we're waitin' for True Romance, I gotta stop somewhere 'n' get me some flies. Ain't no way I ain't gonna get me a piece a' *that* action."

Philo smiled. He took the string of trout from Clyde. "Anybody here hungry?"

ELEVEN

The fish were frying in the pan, and a fresh pot of coffee perked on the grate. As Echo and Orville ate, Philo relaxed against a log. He nursed a cup of coffee, smiling to himself, watching Clyde happily searching for grubs and insects beneath overturned logs and rocks. Clyde rooted intently in the brush, making small hoots of pleasure whenever he found a particularly succulent morsel. Philo watched Clyde abstractly, aware only of the warm sun, tranquillity, and the good feelings that enveloped him. At times, Philo and Clyde shared a distinctly uncomplicated view of the universe.

Fifty yards away, the highway rolled toward Denver. Cars and trucks whizzed past, visible only as blurs through the grove of trees that separated the campsite from the road.

From the west, a Travelall hauling an old Airstream approached the turnoff to the campground. As the vehicle passed a large scrub oak, Lynne Halsey-Taylor sat back, partially hidden in the shadow of the door post. Her eyes flicked apprehensively toward the grove of trees. She could see the Apache parked at the edge of a small clearing. A figure moved beside it. She turned her head away, accelerating. Soon the grove of trees was only a dark speck in the rear-view mirror.

The midday sun scorched the pavement as six highly polished choppers roared east on Highway 66, past gas stations, cafes, cheap motels, and orange groves. A roadside fruit stand flashed by, the lone male clerk serving a host of impatient customers. Fruit orchards gave way to stretches of chaparral and finally sage-covered desert. Twelve dirt-caked, wind-blown Black Widows, riding double on their spitting machines, rolled grim-faced down the highway on an odyssey to regain their manhood. Their mission: to slay the dragon who had cost them half their transportation and too much of their conglomerate pride.

Putnam jockeyed his Jeep through the streets of Santa Fe as though it were a patrol car. He blatantly ignored crosswalks, charging through intersections as lights turned from yellow to red, eliciting comments from irate motorists. Putnam was definitely not a defensive driver, assuming that others would naturally make way for him. It wasn't that he considered himself above the law; such a suggestion would have hurt him deeply. It was simply that he *was* the law.

The Jeep passed through Santa Fe, then rolled north toward Taos. The radio crackled — police calls, Putnam's favourite form of entertainment. Herb was reading out loud from a Triple A brochure.

"It says here," said Herb, "that German brown and local trout abound in nearby streams. During the winter the skiing is excellent."

"Where's this?" asked Putnam.

Herb peered at the brochure and turned the page to look at the map. He ran his finger across it, pinpointing the location. "Not far from Taos." He read from the book, ". . . located between the Rio Grande and the Sangre de Cristo Mountains . . . first discovered by Spaniards in the early seventeenth century. During the summer, a music festival draws hundreds of . . ."

Putnam held up his hand, halting Herb in midsentence. "Herb?"

Herb looked up from the brochure. "Huh?"

"The part about the trout?"

"Yuh?" Herb waited expectantly.

"That was enough."

The bait-and-tackle shop stood near the shore of a small lake, its shelves laden with supplies for the camper, fisherman, and hunter. The Apache was parked in front of the building. Inside, Orville and Echo were replenishing supplies. Orville stood fascinated in front of a wall of tied flies. He could hardly contain himself. He picked up several, gently smoothing their feathered surfaces and gingerly testing their barbed points. Echo was busily engaged in opening jars of fish eggs and other assorted exotic baits, sniffing the contents and making faces.

Orville replaced the flies he held and stepped back to take in the whole display.

"Well, lookit all a' them," he said, pleased. "Have you ever seen so many tied flies in all your born life?"

Echo looked up, preoccupied. She nodded her head, carefully screwing the cap back on a jar.

A Jeep pickup rolled into the parking lot and pulled to a stop near the Apache. Two passengers got out.

Putnam stretched, easing his back muscles. It had been a fair drive. He motioned to Herb. The screen clonked shut behind them.

The clerk nodded to the two men, straightening up from his newspaper. "Help you?" he asked.

Putnam approached and leaned his bulk against the counter. "Where would you say your best trout'd be hidin'?" he asked. He could've been interrogating a hot hit-and-run suspect.

"Maybe four or five miles," replied the clerk mechanically. He volunteered no further information. He looked at Putnam curiously.

"Would you tell us how to get there?" asked Herb.

The clerk's face was a blank. "Up the main highway 'bout

141

three miles, then left at the fork, another mile and a half to the bridge, and then upstream a couple a' hundred yards." His voice sounded like a recording.

"S'cuse me," said Herb. He reached into his pocket for his notebook and pencil. "Would you mind runnin' that down one more time?" He held his pencil poised as Putnam moved away from the counter toward the fly rods.

The monotonous voice of the clerk droned on, repeating the direction for Herb's scribbling pencil. Putnam picked up a rod and tested it expertly, hefting it for balance and gauging the snap. He set the rod back into the rack and picked up another, giving it the same treatment.

"Orville, come lookit this." Echo was holding a bottle of large pickled grubs. "These little humpers look just like the ones Clyde was eatin' this mornin'." She held the bottle toward Orville.

Putnam did a slow take, glancing from Echo to Orville and back again to Echo. His eyes squinted thoughtfully as he quietly replaced the rod.

Orville was engaged in earnest conversation with the owner of a boat-rental yard. Orville pointed at a canoe and smiled. The owner shook his head. More palaver and finally a meeting of the minds. The two men removed a canoe from the rack and carried it to the Apache. Orville tied it down securely on the roof of the camper. He waved as the Apache pulled out onto the highway. Several hundred yards away the Jeep pickup started its engine, pulling onto the highway behind the Apache.

Orville drove several miles up the road, then turned left at a fork. The Jeep kept pace. A mile and a half farther, the Apache came to a bridge, slowed, and turned onto a dirt track, which ran beside a stream. Orville continued on for a hundred yards, then braked the vehicle to a halt.

Putnam and Herb pulled to the shoulder as the Apache slowed to a stop. Putnam turned off the engine. They listened intently, watching, as Orville unloaded supplies. Putnam held his breath.

"Hey, Philo-o-!" Orville's voice cut clearly through the still air.

Putnam turned to Herb, his face wreathed in a grin. Starting the engine, he moved the Jeep onto the dirt track. As they approached the Apache, Putnam saw Philo standing next to Orville. Putnam turned and grinned again, punching Herb's leg in triumph. Herb winced. Putnam continued upstream for a couple of hundred yards, finally pulling off the road high on the slope above the lake. He looked at Herb.

"Okay," he said, "we got 'im. Now we've got to separate him from his friends." Putnam checked his service revolver, spinning the chambers with a practiced thumb. Herb did the same, blowing the dust from the blue steel and carefully wiping the barrel across his shirt. Putnam reached onto the rifle rack and removed a shot-gun. Digging into a bag behind the seat, he grabbed a handful of shells.

"Why the scatter-gun?" asked Herb.

"Don't want to miss," said Putnam. He handed the shotgun to Herb. "You carry it."

The stream joined the lake at the base of the hill, where a small sandy spit jutted out into the lake waters. Dense brush hid the spot from the road that wound upward from the bridge. Dragon-flies flitted through the tangle of shrubs, resting momentarily, then scooting across the water on translucent wings. A squirrel chattered noisily from a stunted pine.

Philo was naked, enjoying the feel of the sun on his body. He stood on the bank, rod in hand, lazily casting into the clear water. He reeled in and cast again. On the bank beside him lay three huge trout. Far out on the lake, Philo could see the canoe, paddles flashing. He hummed softly to himself, satisfied.

Well out of sight and several hundred yards from Philo, Putnam and Herb waited.

Finally, Putnam nodded. Herb, shotgun in hand, started

back down the dirt road.

"Hold on a minit," said Putnam. He walked to the back of the Jeep and unloaded his fishing gear. "Better we take some fishing tackle."

Herb stopped. He looked at Putnam questioningly. "Oh?"

Putnam nodded sagely, tapping his head. "There just might be somebody else around."

Gathering their gear, the two men walked toward the stream. The lake came into view. Putnam stopped his companion and pointed. The canoe was halfway across the lake. The two men could hear the faint sound of the paddles and Orville and Echo's laughter wafting through the stillness. A bee buzzed close and Herb slapped at it viciously. Putnam brought his fingers to his lips with a frown.

"I'm goin' straight on ahead," whispered Putnam. He checked his revolver again, spinning the cylinder. "You circle around and come up behind him."

Herb shook the shotgun in agreement and slipped into the underbrush. Putnam forged ahead stealthily.

Cutting across the bank, Putnam eased himself through the brush and headed downstream. He cursed silently as his foot dislodged a stone, sending it clattering to the rocks several feet below. He stumbled. Steadying himself, he peered through the brush ahead of him. Nothing. A stick snapped beneath his weight. He crouched low, holding his breath. Silence. He moved ahead, conscious of a vague ringing in his ears and the muffled sounds of his own rapid heartbeat. He paused at the base of a small scrub oak and took several deep breaths. Through the brush he could see the clear expanse of blue. A fly settled on his nose. He brushed at it ineffectively. Putnam choked back a sneeze. Putnam waited a few moments; then, hearing nothing, he started off again. The lake grew closer. Putnam's heart beat faster. He was stalking his prey.

Bending low, Putnam pushed aside a stand of brush. Standing on the bank of the stream was a naked figure.

Philo cast, feeling the satisfactory whip of the rod. The

line curled into midstream. He reeled in, stripped off a dozen feet, and let the hook drift. Another cast, this time to the opposite bank. The line arched into a placid pool beneath the roots of a gnarled oak.

"Stinkin' hippie," Putnam mouthed as he watched Philo. Then he saw the three huge trout on the bank. Jesus H. Christ!, he thought, those suckers were the biggest he'd ever seen. He leaned forward to get a better view, momentarily forgetting Philo. He shook his head. Those monsters must have put up one hell of a fight. Goddamn! Sure would be nice to tie into one of those mothers. Putnam could *feel* a trout like that on his line.

The sound of the reel brought Putnam back. He settled himself in the bushes to wait. Damn that Herb, he thought, where the hell is he?

Herb, leaving Putnam, crossed into the underbrush and made his way downstream, taking advantage of the thick chaparral and mesquite that grew alongside the hill. Struggling upward, he stopped to get his bearings. He could see the lake to the right and below him the stream. Somewhere ahead, hidden by the undergrowth, the stream fed into the lake. From this height, Herb could look down and see anything that moved. Nothing.

Catching his breath, Herb crossed a bare patch of shale. He slipped and slid in the loose rocks. Righting himself, he leaned on the shotgun for support. Gingerly, he eased onto a rock outcropping and sat down heavily, breathing hard. Philo Beddoe was probably just below him. Sure were goin' to have some fun when they caught up with that turkey, he thought. Herb took another step, then froze, his curly hair damn near straight! There was no mistaking that sound!

Sweat broke out on Herb's face in glassy globules. "Who's that . . .?" he moaned, his eyes wide with horror. The sound seemed to come from everywhere. "Don't tell me," he groaned. "I know . . ." And his eyes focussed on the biggest, meanest-looking rattler he'd ever had a nightmare about. It was coiled less than two feet from his face, rattle vibrating like a buzz saw, forked tongue flicking wickedly. They were damn near eyeball to eyeball.

"Ooh . . .," said Herb in a small voice. "*You* are U-G-L-Y!" The snake looked back at him. Herb blanched.

Carefully, he brought up the shotgun. It seemed to take hours. Finally the barrel was pointed at the snake's head. Herb released the safety and winced at the loud click. The snake continued to vibrate. Herb started to squeeze the trigger.

"Shit!" The expletive slid from his mouth in a quiet hiss. He eased off the trigger. If he blew the rattler's head off, he'd also blow any chance of taking Philo Beddoe by surprise. The sweat dripped off him. He wanted to piss. An unmoving statue, he waited.

From his hiding place deep in the bushes, Putnam anxiously checked his watch. There was still no sign of Herb. Where was that dumb shit? he thought. Putnam chewed at his lip impatiently as Philo changed flies. Christ! What was taking Herb so long? Putnam drummed his fingers against the butt of his revolver. Philo cast upstream, his fly bouncing in the churning water. Damnit, Putnam thought, there wasn't any point in waiting. That son-ofabitch must have got himself lost.

Putnam drew his revolver and stepped from the bushes. He aimed the cold steel at Philo's back. His heart pounded in excitement.

"You so much as blink," Putnam's voice was curt with authority and anger, "and I'm gonna blow your balls off." He cocked the hammer.

Philo froze. He heard the click of the hammer and was a believer. Holding the rod stiffly in front of him, he felt his mouth go dry. Philo licked his lips and without turning his head, spoke.

"Who are you . . .?" No answer. "What do you want?"

Putnam eased up behind him, the revolver uncertain. "Just don't you move." Putnam's voice was cold and hard.

"You'll find out soon enough." He took another step toward Philo, his mouth set. He had the sonofabitch, he thought triumphantly, right where he wanted him. Putnam toyed with the idea of pulling the trigger. This asshole was finally going to get his. Hell yes! And there wasn't a damn thing the naked shithead could do about it. Putnam savoured the moment.

"Jesus H. Christ!" Philo's voice shattered the silence as a trout struck the lure. The tip of the rod bent to the surface of the water. The reel sang as yards of line disappeared into the stream. "Sonofabitch must weigh six pounds!" Philo yelled, Putnam momentarily forgotten.

Putnam watched in fascination as the line rapidly reversed direction and dashed upstream. Then the fish broke the surface, leaping a good two feet in the air.

"Holy shit!" Putnam gasped.

Philo waded into the shallows and began reeling in the slack as the trout raced downstream again.

"Don't move!" ordered Putnam, trying to keep his eyes on Philo and still follow the progress of the fish.

"What the hell do you expect me to do with him?" The rod bent double as the trout took up the line and fought the drag.

"Just keep your hands up and don't turn around!"

Philo complied, holding the twisting, jumping rod in one hand. He stood immobile, his face reflecting his frustration.

Putnam waded into the water behind Philo, his eyes gleaming. The reel hummed out another twenty feet of line. "Give me that rod!" The revolver wavered.

Philo started to turn.

"DON'T TURN AROUND, GODDAMNIT!" Putnam shouted the words into Philo's ear.

Philo carefully handed the bending rod behind him. He didn't look around.

Ferociously, Putnam grabbed the rod with his right hand and braced the cork heel against his thigh. Standing in the shallows, gun in one hand, rod in the other, Putnam

147

tightened the drag with his thumb. The trout was pulling like a sonofabitch. Putnam looked at the revolver. Decisions.

Herb's eyes stung, blurring momentarily. He blinked to clear them. Sweat rolled off his forehead. The reptile reared back, rattling. Then it slithered closer. "Oh shit!" Herb's mind raced, on the verge of panic. The snake stopped, observing him with opaque eyes. The rattler's head was less than a foot away. Ever so gently, Herb raised the shotgun, carefully clicking on the safety. The rattler's tail vibrated again.

In one swift movement Herb brought the shotgun crashing down on the triangular-shaped head. The viper thrashed, lashing its body in its death throes, its rattle still upright and buzzing. Herb wiped his face, still trembling, and stepped back, drenched with sweat. Grimacing with loathing, he lifted the writhing, crushed thing with the barrel of the shotgun and heaved it far into the underbrush.

Moving quickly to make up time, Herb crossed the hill and headed toward the mouth of the stream. Tripping over a branch, he tumbled head first into a patch of poison oak. Cursing, he got up slowly. Peering at the shrubs, he groaned, recognising the familiar shape of the leaves. Herb jumped to his feet, wiping his contaminated hands on his clothes. Gingerly, he picked up the shotgun and fly rod. He was beginning to itch already.

The fish flashed to the surface again, clearing the water with a mighty snap of tail. Putnam, his mouth agape, jerked back on the rod, his pistol waving. "It's a sonofabitchin' monster!" he yelled.

"If you don't mind my askin'," said Philo, still frozen, "what the hell is goin' on?"

"Shut up!" Putnam barked excitedly. The feel of the fish on the line was too much for him. He jammed the gun into his belt and shifted the rod to his left hand, reeling in the slack, playing the huge fish. Philo heard him grunt with the exertion.

From the corner of his eye, Philo noted the movements of the rod. He heard the click of the reel as Putnam frantically turned it. No one could do that and still hold a gun unless he had three hands. The line snaked in, leaving pearly drops at the tip of the rod. The trout began to tire as Putnam, the consummate sportsman, played the fish closer and closer. The trout jumped again, still game, fighting the unrelenting barb in its mouth.

Putnam was breathing hard, eyes only for the silvery-brown fish. "I've never seen anything like it!" he gasped. The trout was almost to Philo's feet, still battling, but no match for the excited Putnam.

Philo's move was so sudden that Putnam had no time to react. Grabbing the line, Philo jerked the fish free of the water and in the same motion whirled around. Six pounds of trout swung in a wide arc, smashing full bore into Putnam's face. He dropped the rod and fell backward. In an instant Philo was on him. Two quick punches and it was over. Putnam's head lolled in the shallow water. The trout, freed by the force of the blow, swam reprieved past his unseeing eyes.

Philo hauled Putnam onto the bank. He stared at him for a long moment, then dragged him up and over the rocks, into the brush. Roughly, he propped the soaking Putnam against the trunk of a willow, and remembering, he waited.

Herb made his way to the base of the hill and stopped. He listened; no sound except the waters of the lake gently lapping at the shore. He poked his head through the bushes. Philo was gone. Far out on the lake, Herb could see the canoe. Cautiously he worked his way through the brush and approached the stream. His hands and face itched voraciously. He clawed at himself miserably. No sign of anybody. Tentatively, he called out in a whisper. "Putnam . . . Putnam . . . Where are you?" No answer. Only the rustling of the leaves. Herb waited a moment, then tried again, louder this time. "Putnam . . . Where are you?" Silence. Nervously Herb checked the load in the shotgun and released the safety. Something was wrong. He itched off through the bush, skirting the stream. Now he was the hunter. The instinct that carried Stone Age man down these same paths was not dead. He felt the danger and excitement. His heart pounded as he called out again. "Putnam, it's me . . . Herb. Where are you?" A note of fear crept into his voice. The silence about him was over-powering. The shrubs, trees, and even the sky pressed in on him. Herb moved farther into the brush, stopping every few seconds to look, scartch, and listen.

Herb broke into a small clearing near the bank of the stream. Something caught his eye at the base of a willow. He peered across the clearing. It was most definitely a boot. Herb quickly crossed the clearing. Putnam was half hidden in the weeds. "Putnam!" Herb dropped to his knees beside his prostrate partner.

From high in the willow, the naked form dropped. Herb screamed. The shotgun went flying as Herb fell under a rain of sledgehammer blows. With practiced precision, Philo methodically beat the living shit out of him. Moments later, two unconscious forms were stretched peacefully in the shade.

Out on the lake, Orville and Echo were fishing. A string of trout and crappies lay in the centre of the canoe. Suddenly from across the placid water came a sound that sent chills through both of them. They sat up abruptly.

"AHHH - AHHH - AHH - EEEEE - EE - OWWW!" The victory cry of the great apes pierced through the stillness.

"What in hell is that?!" asked Echo. She looked at Orville in amazement.

Orville looked toward the shore and winced.

"That sounded just like . . ." Echo continued.

"Sometimes," said Orville, "I think he spends too much time with Clyde."

TWELVE

Gathering the assorted firearms that Putnam and Herb were carrying, Philo made his way back to the Jeep. Carrying the rifles and shells from the cab, he hurled them far out into the lake. Then, grim-faced, he returned to the Jeep and started it up.

Backing the pickup down the road some fifty yards, Philo gunned the engine. Holding the door open, he tromped the accelerator to the floor, guiding the Jeep up and off the road toward the lake. He was doing forty when he reached the embankment. Philo gave it one last tromp, then kicked it out of gear. He jumped, rolling free. The Jeep careened down the hill, up a slight rise, then tumbled over the precipice. It bounced once, landing with a great splash some thirty yards into the lake.

The truck settled slowly, the water rushing up and over the bumpers. The front end nosed down as the cab filled. Then the Jeep disappeared beneath the surface with a burp and a belch. It bubbled for a few minutes, and then the waters were calm.

The portable radio was blaring. Philo was combing Clyde's long red hair. It was dusk, almost time to meet Lynne. Philo whistled to himself, happy at the thought of seeing her again. Clyde grunted amiably as the comb snagged a hunk of matted hair. The ape scratched under his armpit, carefully popping whatever he found into his mouth.

It had been a helluva day, Philo thought, chuckling as he remembered the truck disappearing into the lake. Herb and Putnam were going to have one long walk. He laughed out loud as he gave Clyde the finishing touches. Philo rubbed the animal's head affectionately.

"That should take care of you for a while," he said.

Philo grabbed a towel and headed for the campground showers, holding out his hand as he passed Orville and Echo. Orville reached into a small leather bag and handed him a razor and some soap, then as an added thought a bottle of aftershave. Echo threw him a stick of deodorant. Philo looked at her questioningly. She nodded emphatically, holding her nose.

Showered, shaved, defunked, and deodorized, Philo pulled on his clean clothes. This was going to be one special, extraordinary, incredible evening. He stared at himself in the mirror and grinned. He'd seen a lot worse.

Good tunes boomed from the speakers as the Apache rolled toward Taos. Philo's good feelings were infectious. Orville and Echo clowned, laughing and joking. Philo watched them with amusement and affection. The only thing missing to make it all complete was Lynne Halsey-Taylor. But that would come later. Philo smiled with satisfaction.

The main street of Taos was crowded. Tourists, galleries in abundance, artisans, and Indians. Locals paraded down the cobblestones in jeans, Stetsons, and pointed boots.

The bar in the square was filling up, and the sound of a live band drifted through the clear night air. A country fiddle played counterpoint to a banjo, guitar, and bass. Three Indian youths, long-haired with colourful bandanna sweatbands, stood at the door tapping their feet and ogling girls. The great inverted bowl of the sky sparkled with lights and oulined the sacred Taos mountain in the distance.

Arm in arm, Philo, Orville, and Echo turned into a Mexican restaurant.

"This the place?" asked Orville.

Philo nodded. "She'll be meetin' us here."

A smiling hostess dressed in full skirt and peasant blouse directed them to a table.

Philo called for beer as the trio studied their menus. Orville ran his finger down the page, pointing ecstatically to almost everything the restaurant had to offer.

Tortillas, chilis, green corn tamales, tacos, enchiladas, Spanish rice, chili rellenos; the dishes smothered the table.

"What are we gonna do with all this food?" Echo asked, buttering a tortilla and stuffing it with chili and vegetables.

"Eat it! All of it!" Philo chomped down on a taco.

"What if I can't?" Echo mumbled, her mouth full.

"Then," said Orville, "we'll just have to give yours t' Clyde."

Philo exploded into laughter.

"What's so funny?" asked Echo. She bit into a relleno.

"Can you imagine," said Philo, "what this stuff would do to his digestive system?" He dropped his fork into the plate and shook his head. Orville and Echo cracked up. "I mean, he already cuts the worst ones I ever heard, and he's never even seen a bean."

The table rocked with laughter.

"Hey," said Orville, recovering from his fit and wiping his mouth with the back of his hand, "what time's yer lady comin'?"

"Won't be too long now." Philo reached across the table to pull over a large tureen of soup. "C'mon, Orville, help me with some of this here *alblondingus*."

Late. The restaurant was empty of customers. The table was cleared, except for doggie bags and a dozen empty beer bottles. The waitress dozed in the corner.

Philo stared morosely at the bottle in his hand. Absently he peeled off the label, crumpling it into a ball and dropping it onto the table. He looked at Orville and Echo, then back at the bottle. He drained it and placed it carefully alongside the dead ones, his face grim. Orville said nothing. He touched Echo's hand, feeling Philo's pain, watching his silent fury.

They drove back to the campground in silence, the radio mute. Philo stared into the darkness.

Orville twisted in the seat uncomfortably. The stillness screamed at him.

"Philo?" Orville ventured the question tentatively. The darkness answered him. He waited a moment before continuing. "Are we . . . uh . . . goin' back?"

Philo's face a mask. Then, finally, "Hell no!" The curt syllables chopped through the stillness. Silence again. Then slowly, and with great precison, "Next time when I find her, I'll do him my way."

The storm rolled out of the Rockies, a grey mass of thunderheads that blanketed three states with an unseasonable chill. It punched south into New Mexico, bringing rain and a dense shroud of clammy fog. Through it, the Apache sped north for Denver.

The windshield wipers sloshed back and forth rhythmically. The dreariness of the day accentuated the sombre mood in the Apache. A plaintive ballad of lost love wailed from the speakers. Philo shut it off. The rain beat down, obscuring the road ahead. Philo cursed the semi that passed for the crescendo of muddy water it threw on his windshield.

The Apache crossed the New Mexico-Colorado border and pulled into a small town. One cafe, grimy; a large sign urging "EAT." It was thirty feet from the truck to the door. They were soaked by the time they stepped inside. Lukewarm coffee, bad food, and rotten service. The juke groaned a lament. Someone "Feelin' Bad." Water dripped down Philo's pants legs into his boots. The bill came; overpriced. Philo paid. A nickel tip. No sign of letup, only drizzle and more rain.

They ran for the truck and piled, in, tired and wet. Nothing on the radio but news and weather; all bad. The Apache turned onto the highway. Three hundred miles to Denver.

Echo settled herself in Orville's arms and closed her eyes. In a few minutes they were both asleep. Philo drove on, his mind a hundred miles and two days back. A sharp knock against the cab's rear window. A hairy hand rapped again. Reaching under the seat. Philo found a beer. He pulled the tab, slid open the window, and handed Clyde the brew.

A cold, wet, and bedraggled dozen rode into Taos on six dripping motorcycles. They circled the square and reined up in front of a cafe. Cholla dismounted, leading the sopping pack into the warmth of the eatery. Subdued by the weather, they crammed themselves around three small tables. Coffee all around. The waitress flung menus at them, angry at the wet the Widows brought in. Two Indians sitting in a booth watched impassively.

Elmo shivered, his hands wrapped around his cup. "Cholla, I been thinkin'," he hesitated, then hurriedly continued before Cholla could make the inevitable reply. "How do we know that old man told us the truth 'bout where this chick's goin'?"

"We don't know," said Cholla.

"Then ain't this a long way to come on just an old man's bullshit?"

"Got mor'n just bullshit." He emptied his fourth sugar into his cup.

"Watcha talkin' about?" interjected Frank. He pulled his chair closer, slurping at his hot liquid.

Cholla daintily took a sip of his coffee and paused for the kick. "If he told us the truth, he may only lose a pound or two." He reached into his leather jacket and withdrew a Kleenex-wrapped object. "If he lied" — Cholla unwrapped the Kleenex — "he's gonna starve to death."

Sitting on the table, with a disembodied grin, were the

old man's dentures.

Somewhere ahead, twisting around sharp curves in the Colorado mountains, a Travelall hauling a trailer sloshed through the driving rain. The driver, eyes riveted to the broken yellow line dividing the highway, hummed an old Edy Lynne tune.

Dusk and many miles to go. The rain turned to hail and made driving difficult. Philo pulled up before a small motel. Its orange sign announcing VACANCY flickered in the wetness. Philo squinted through the windshield to read the price beneath the blinking letters. He nodded.

"I'm tired of being out in this," he said. "What say to a bit of civilisation tonight?"

"If that includes a hot bath," said Echo, "I'm with you."

Orville grunted agreement, then added, "It's gettin' kinda damp fer Clyde back there, too, ain't it?"

Philo looked toward the rear. "If he ain't drownin', he'll wait till bedtime. This time we better sneak him in."

Orville chuckled. "Jest don't forget who's sleepin' with who."

Philo smiled. He was feeling better already. He honked the horn. The manager, disguised in curlers and a slicker, stepped out. Philo rolled down the window. She took his money and pointed to the end of a line of cottages.

The Apache hadn't rolled to a stop before the rumble of motorcycles echoed in the streets. Six Harley choppers, three abreast, zoomed past the sign, which now read NO VACANCY. On the bikes twelve Black Widows hunched miserably in the weather.

The morning dawned pink, clear, and beautiful. The storm had passed, leaving a clean, fresh crispness in its wake. Puddles steamed in the early-morning sun.

The Travelall and trailer were parked in a campground beside a rushing stream. Outside the trailer, Lynne

Halsey-Taylor finished her coffee. She rinsed the cup with some fresh brew from the pot, then dumped both onto the ground. Pot and cup disappeared into a sack, which Lynn tossed into the back of the Travelall.

"Hey," she yelled in the direction of the trailer, "I'm movin' out." No response. She shrugged. She let it warm up for a minute, then pulled away. A sign on the shoulder of the road read, WATCH FOR FALLING ROCKS.

Six choppers ate the miles. Twelve Black Widows, sun-dried and wind-blown, leaned into the corners. A roadside campground flashed past. A sign on the shoulder of the road read, WATCH FOR FALLING ROCKS.

The outskirts of Georgetown, a small Colorado mining community. Lynne Halsey-Taylor pulled into a service station for gas. She stretched her legs while the attendant filled the tank. She'd been driving a long time.

Back on the road again, the Travelall gathered speed as twelve Black Widows passed on the left. The last rider, Bruno, saw the truck, put it all together, and let out a shout. Thundering to the head of the pack he yelled at Cholla, pointing to the trailer coming up behind them. "An Airstream!" He waved wildly. "It's her. That's the one!"

Cholla held up his hand. The bikes slowed and turned, heading back toward the Travelall. Cholla pulled a slip of paper from his pocket. He checked the licence and nodded. Sure was her! The bikes flanked the truck on all sides, forcing Lynne to the shoulder of the road, circling her until she stopped.

Cholla eased up to the driver's side. He tipped his hat to the lady behind the wheel. Cholla smiled. "How do," he said.

He saw her smile, uneasy but not frightened. He didn't see the shotgun pointed at the back of his head from the window of the Travelall.

Cholla consulted his scrap of paper again. "I bet you're

159

Lynne Halsey-Taylor," he said.

Surprised, Lynne smiled openly. "How do you know that?"

Cholla leaned toward the window. The shotgun followed him. "Well, to tell you the truth, we been following you all the way from Los Angeles."

Lynne softened, her voice sexy. "You see me sing at the Palomino?"

"Sorry to say I missed it," apologized Cholla. The safety on the shotgun clicked off. "However, I promise I'll never miss it again." He was all charm.

Lynne relaxed. She looked at Cholla curiously. "What'd all you boys follow me to Colorado for?" Her eyes took in the ranks of Widows surrounding the Travelall.

Cholla tapped his riding crop against his tank. "There's a guy named Philo . . . Philo Beddoe comin' after you. You know that?"

Lynne nodded. She bit her lower lip nervously. "Yes . . . yes, I know that."

"You a friend of his?" asked Cholla.

"Not particularly," said Lynne. The bikers listened intently.

"You want to see him?" Cholla scratched his ear.

"Not particularly," she said.

Cholla looked at her. His eyes narrowed. He smiled. "We do." The shotgun disappeared from the trailer window.

The spectacular Rockies: Deep gorges, rushing white-water streams, tall pines and aspens, sparkling greens and blues flashed by in a haze of colour. The Apache's ever-present radio sang of sweet valleys and gentle people.

Twenty miles and several songs later, Philo crossed the tiny bridge spanning the roaring, churning stream, past the sign that read, WELCOME TO GEORGETOWN, COLORADO.

Quaint Victorian gingerbread houses, boardwalks, and belly-up bars. Store-front windows, gold pans, hurricane

160

lamps, and antique bottles reflecting blues and browns in the afternoon sun. A town born of the mother lode — bred from the silver in its hills, a splinter of the past.

Now the silver was gone, replaced by tourist gold.

A huge trash truck rumbled down Main Street, making its weekly pickup. It stopped at a trash bin and inserted large forks into receptacles beneath the steel box. With a grinding of gears, the forks lifted the bin high overhead, emptying the contents into the compactor at the rear. A loud crunching compacted the trash inside as the forks returned the empty bin to the street.

Philo drove slowly past the dumpster. Orville watched in fascination as the machine methodically performed its tasks. His tow truck had given him a respect for the power of the machine. He whistled softly as another bin rose high into the air, dumped a load, then gently settled to the ground. It was impressive.

The Apache rolled down Main Street. A silver trailer was parked by the hotel. In front of it, the familiar Travelall.

Philo jammed on the brakes. "There she is!" he yelled. He didn't notice the six motorcycles parked down and across the street. He pulled over and jumped out. Orville started to slide out, but Philo stopped him.

"Orville, you stay here. This is personal."

Orville shrugged.

Philo walked over to the Travelall. It was empty and locked. He knocked at the trailer door. He tried the handle. It was locked. Philo looked up and down the street.

Some hundred yards away, a couple walked out of the combination cafe, filling station, and general store. The girl looked mighty like Lynne Halsey-Taylor. Philo started to call out, then, thinking better of it, walked quickly toward them. The couple crossed the tiny street and stepped into an alley whose buildings fronted on Main Street.

Philo was half running when he reached the alley. He turned in and stopped. There was no sign of the girl or her companion.

The trash truck moved past the Apache and came to a halt. The driver climbed down from his cab and walked to the cafe. Coffee time. Orville looked at the behemoth, his eyes bright with curiosity. He turned to Echo.

"Hang on there fer a minute," he said. "I got to check that thing out." Echo nodded sleepily as Orville walked over to the compactor. He patted its sides respectfully, then climbed up on the running board to take a look inside.

Philo started down the alley looking for Lynne. Three denim-and-leather-clad figures stepped from the shadows to block the far end. Philo stopped, his hackles rising.

The jackbooted figure whacked his riding crop against his boot top.

"You Philo Beddoe?" His voice was crisp and menacing.

"Do I know you?" Philo's eyes were wary, his voice taut.

"You're gonna," said Cholla, his quirt rattling. Another Widow ventured forward. "Philo Beddoe, your time has come." Woody flipped up his eye patch and stared at Philo across a large mud puddle.

"I know *you*," Philo said. "Last time we met you were catchin' a fast freight."

Two Widows slunk from the street to block the alley behind Philo. Seven more emerged from various nooks and crannies. Slowly they advanced. Philo looked around. He knew what was going to happen and only wished there were two more of him. Skirting the puddle, he walked toward Cholla. Frank jumped between them, mumbling an obscenity. He wanted first.

Orville, unable to resist the blandishments of the trasher, opened the door and climbed in. Happily he sat at the controls, observing and touching the various levers and gears. He turned and motioned for Echo to come over and look. Echo shook her head, primping in the rear-view mirror. Orville turned back to his clinical examination of the trasher's intricacies.

In the alley, surrounded by the twelve Widows, Philo listened gravely to Frank's epithets. He was aware that the

162

dialogue was the accepted prelude to battle. Philo considered which Widow to eliminate first. The decision was suddenly taken out of his hands.

Frank, running out of things to say, looped a wild right at Philo's head. Philo blocked the blow, and dropped Frank and three others. Sidling up from the rear, Bruno levied a cruncher. Philo turned and sent him flying into the mud. None of the Widows were prepared for the grizzly fury they had bitten into. Philo's arms were pile-driving pistons wreaking havoc on their bodies. An elbow to the gut sent one of them sliding into the dirt. Another's head snapped and popped and he collapsed into a growing, moaning pile of bikers.

The sound of battle reached Orville. The alley was now a mass of kicking, cursing bodies. It took Orville a moment to realise what was going on. Then, seeing the six bikes parked on the street, his mind clicked. It all came together. Kicking the trasher into life, he lowered the forks and headed for the nearest bike. The prongs caught the machine midspokes. Orville rammed a lever and the forks rose, carrying the bike up and over the cab. It dropped with a crash into the compactor. Orville punched a button and hydraulically reduced the chopper to scrap. He growled for the next bike.

Philo was not faring too badly, considering the odds. Three Widows had literally bitten the dust and another was still retching his guts out. With four of their number down, the Widows tore into Philo in earnest. The bikers charged, fists and feet flying. Philo met two head on, shaking off blows. A left across the eyes sent one careening into a row of trash cans. Another screamed as Philo's knee caught him in the balls. He jumped away howling, holding himself tenderly. Three downed bikers, coming back to life, staggered to their feet, cleared their heads, and piled in, this time more cautiously.

Orville was getting the hang of the machine. Efficiently the prong pierced two choppers. Another pull and the Harleys disappeared into the innards of the truck. The hydraulic ram slid forward again.

Unnoticed, the Travelall started up. With scarcely a glance at the marauding trasher or the mayhem in the alley, Lynne Halsey-Taylor moved down the street. She was up to speed by the time the trailer rolled past the sign that read, LEAVING GEORGETOWN—A FRIENDLY PLACE.

Another bike joined its companions in the bowels of the trasher. Orville was enjoying himself immensely. He'd mastered a dive-and-swoop technique that kept the trasher moving and chewing at the same time.

The Widows were so immersed in battle that the noise of the grinding and scrunching of their machines couldn't distract them. Philo lashed out again and again, connecting, but beginning to tire.

Cholla, with his usual foresight, managed for the most part to stay clear of the action, limiting his participation to various yells, stances, and words of encouragement. Philo, after damn near twisting Dallas's horned head from his body, unceremoniously dumped Elmo into a garbage can.

Cholla winced as Elmo emerged and fainted.

Turning his head with the shame of it all, Cholla saw his worst nightmare coming true. While the trasher chewed and spit hunks of chrome and fender, the last of the Harleys, Elmo's three-wheeler, dangled on the forks of the monster.

"AAAHHHHHHHHHH!!!!!!! LOOK" Cholla screamed. "The bikes! The bikes! Get the bikes!"

The Widows turned and as a body let out a howl of anguish. The last bike hung precariously in midair. With maddened screams the group turned from the alley and raced for the trasher, tromping Cholla into the mud en route.

With the furious Widows scrambling toward him, Orville figured it was time to leave. He rammed the lever, dropping both the forks and the cycle. The bike bounced as it hit the ground, then crumpled in the dust. Orville hit the ground simultaneously and started running. He wasn't sure where to, but anywhere else was preferable. The mangled Widows clamoured in hot pursuit.

Echo, having watched the entire debacle in awe and disbelief, saw Orville leap from the trasher, followed by the howling bikers. They were unquestionably bent on murdering her man. Sliding behind the wheel, she cranked the Apache over and squealed down the street. She passed the pounding Widows and pulled alongside Orville, who was running like a bandit.

"Hey," she called out, "would you like a ride?"

Orville was in no mood. "Jesus Christ," he yelled, "get the hell over here."

The closest Widow made a flying leap for Orville. The Widow missed by a fingernail, falling flat on his face.

Echo swerved closer and Orville grabbed the rear-view mirror. Catching it, he swung onto the running board. Another biker swung up behind Orville. Orville's boot sent him flying. With a leap reminiscent of Burt Lancaster, Elmo landed on the back step of the camper and held on for dear life. As he hung there, it occurred to him to simply go through the camper and attack Orville from the rear.

Elmo opened the camper and swung in. The door slammed behind him. Five long, hairy fingers at the end of a fifty-two-inch arm encircled his head, pulling him . . . to the sweetest mouth this side of Sumatra.

"AAAAARRRGGGGHHHHH AAAHHHHHHH-HHH!!!!!" Elmo's screams reverberated through the camper and echoed down the street. The camper blasted open and Elmo came flying out. He hit the asphalt with a scream, rolling down the street. From the rear of the Apache, an excited Clyde jumped up and down, bashing at the floor, hooting at the top of his lungs. The door flapped open, slammed closed, then flapped open again. With a huge simian grin, Clyde reached into the Colorado sunshine and flipped the pursuing Windows an eight-inch bird.

Echo pulled alongside the alley. Philo hopped into the truck as Echo slid over.

"What took ya so long?" he asked. Philo tried to smile but

the effort hurt. They all cracked up. Philo floored it and roared out of Georgetown, leaving twelve war-weary Widows standing devastated in the Apache's dust.

THIRTEEN

The Travelall swung through Idaho Springs, a tiny mountain town; around twisting mountain roads, past old silver mines, and spanking new ski resorts that promised the best powder in the world, come winter. Lynne handled the Travelall and trailer as though they were extensions of herself. She smiled at the song on the radio, then sang softly, in harmony with the tune. She echoed the refrain, "Coming Home."

At a crossroads, Philo pulled over to the side. "'Pears we have a choice," he said. He pulled a map from the glove compartment and studied it carefully. "Looks like that one leads to Denver." Philo pointed.

Orville looked over his shoulder, "And that one, and that one."

After careful scrutiny, each one chose a different direction. "Looks like Clyde will have to settle it," said Philo. They each threw a match of a different size into a sack and handed it back to Clyde. The ape studied the sack with interest, then reached in and pulled out one of the matches.

"That way," said Orville.

A sign pointing in another direction read, IDAHO SPRINGS, 23 MILES.

The Travelall entered Denver from the west, cruising the streets like a homing pigeon headed for its coop. The vehicle passed the used-car lots of West Denver, the mile-high home of the Denver Broncos, then crossed town and headed east for Aurora. It was late when Lynne turned off East Colfax and into her trailer court. She stopped in front of the neon sign that read OFFICE. Lynne Halsey-Taylor was home.

Entering Denver from the south, Philo rolled past the skeletons of newly framed condos pushing aside brick and frame houses, filling the pastures of yesterday. Turning off the expressway, he swung onto a main thoroughfare and chose the nearest motel.

Philo woke early, Orville and Echo were still asleep. Philo shaved and dressed quickly. Slipping the Denver Yellow Pages under his arm, Philo quietly left the room and climbed into the Apache. Once in the truck, he marked several mobile-home parks. Working carefully from a map, he circled their locations. Thirty minutes later he was at the first one.

The old lady behind the counter surveyed Philo suspiciously.

"You lookin' for somebody or just sight-seein'?"

"Lookin' for somebody," said Philo, "girl by the name a' Lynne Halsey-Taylor, driving a Travelall haulin' a silver Airstream?"

"Nope," replied the old lady, "ain't never had no Halsey-Taylors."

"A Schyler maybe?"

"Never had none a' them kind either. Somethin' like a Airstream?"

Philo shook his head, heading for the door.

Philo drove rapidly out of the court.

Several trailer parks later, Philo pulled the Apache to the side of the road. He cracked two beers and handed one to Clyde. "Not doin' too good, are we, partner?" Philo pulled out the map again and scratched off another circle. He finished his beer.

It was several hours before Philo returned to the motel. Orville and Echo were just stepping out. From the look on Philo's face, Orville could see that he hadn't had any luck.

"We thought we'd get some dinner," said Orville. "You want to come?"

"Naw, I'll feed Clyde 'n' me later." Philo leaned against the steering wheel.

"We could bring ya some chicken," said Echo.

Philo shook his head.

When he had showered, shaved, and changed, it was dark. A bout with the Yellow Pages and map, then into the Apache, heading for downtown Denver. The garish sign before him proclaimed there had been better days for the BROKEN SPUR. He parked in front of the seedy-looking bar and entered. The tavern was dimly lit. There were few customers. Philo spun himself onto a stool and ordered a Coors. Country music was playing on the jukebox.

"Do you have a New-talent Night?"

The bartender brought the beer. "What's that?" He carefully wiped a glass and stacked it with several others.

"Bands and singers . . . stuff like that?" Philo looked around the room, noting the absence of anything that looked like action.

"Oh yeh. I know what you mean." The bartender continued to clean glasses. He volunteered no further information.

"Well, do you?" Philo was getting impatient.

"Nope," said the bartender, "just the box."

Philo curbed the impatience. "You know another place that has live music?"

"A couple," said the bartender. "The best one's the Zanzibar, in Aurora." He turned back to his glasses, and a sink of soapy water.

"Do you know a Tank Murdoch?" asked Philo.

"Sure do," said the bartender, interested. "You lookin' for him?"

Philo took a long swallow of beer. "Yeh."

The bartender looked at Philo appraisingly. "You got a beef? Never knew nobody ever lookin' to find *him*."

Philo shrugged. "You know where he is?"

The bartender smiled. "Just keep askin'. He'll find you."

Philo turned the truck around and headed east, toward Aurora. A twenty-minute drive found him circling the Zanzibar. Cars jammed the parking lot. He found a space and walked in.

The Zanzibar could have been a country-western club anywhere: the same kind of people, the same kind of talk; on the stage, the same music. Hearing it made Philo feel at home. That's the kind of music it was. Philo moved to the bar and called for a beer. He looked around. Badly painted scenes of cowboys and their stories cluttered the walls in iridescent green and orange.

"When's your New-talent Night?" he asked when the bartender set the bottle down.

"You sing?" The bartender looked at Philo doubtfully.

"Nope. A friend of mine does."

"Seems nowadays," the bartender reflected, "everybody sings." Apparently he thought there were too many.

"Maybe you know her," said Philo. "Lynne Halsey-Taylor?"

"Brunette. Green eyes, pretty little thing?"

"That's her," said Philo. He tipped the neck of the bottle toward the bartender.

The man thought for a moment. "Ain't seen her for a while."

"She's been out of town." Philo finished the beer and asked for another.

"She came in a lot."

Philo nodded. "When is it?"

"When is what?" asked the bartender.

172

"Your New-talent Night."

"Oh," said the bartender. "Tomorrow."

Philo thoughtfully finished the second bottle.

Tomorrow came. Orville, Echo, and Philo were travelling Aurora, east. The Zanzibar Club loomed ahead of them. Philo cut the radio, slowing for a blinking yellow.

"You sure you don't want me to just stick around outta sight, sorta? I mean, he did go kinda crazy with a shotgun once." Orville looked at Philo with concern.

"Nope," said Philo. "I 'preciate your thinkin' but I gotta go this one alone."

Orville shrugged. "How 'bout if Echo 'n' me just hung out for a beer and to hear the sounds . . .?" He looked up hopefully.

"Uh-uh!"

"Borrow my peashooter?" asked Echo.

Philo smiled at her and shook his head. "Thanks, no." He pulled the Apache to a stop in front of the huge neon sign reading "ZANZIBAR — Enjoy yourself, it's later than you think."

"They got another one of these places on Larimer Street in downtown Denver," Philo said. "Why'n't you guys check it out?"

Orville scooted into the driver's seat.

Philo started to turn away, then remembered. "Oh yeah . . . Tank Murdoch is around."

Orville nodded, absorbing the information. "Take care, huh?"

Philo winked, waved a get-going, and strode into the club.

The place was full. Philo paid his cover and beckoned to the waitress. He asked for a table: the kind they always give you when you don't want it, in the back, behind a post. She looked at him funny and led him through the smoke and darkness. He ordered a pitcher.

The group onstage finished and the emcee asked for more

173

applause.

The emcee cleared his throat and looked around the room. "And now, while Hossfat is taking their break, the Thursday-night policy at the Zanzibar is to give a chance to new and upcoming talent. Some of them, you may have heard here before, and we hope that you'll be hearing from all of 'em again! The first is a young man passin' through from Nashville on his way to Holleewood. Let's give a nice welcome to Nashville's own Harlan Toothacker!"

The emcee stepped back as a large, Levi's-clad young man mounted the stage carrying a mother-of-pearl, engraved Gibson guitar. The crowd applauded politely. He acknowledged them with a grin and started to sing. Philo looked around the room, not listening to the words and only vaguely aware of the music.

Two acts later Philo finished the pitcher. The two sisters onstage stepped down to sparse applause. The waitress came to the table.

"Want another one?"

"No," said Philo. He smiled at the girl.

"Did you know that we have a buffet tonight?" She emptied the ashtray and replaced it with another one. "All you can eat for only $3.95. The entrée is prime rib."

"Thanks, no," Philo continued smiling. "This'll be fine."

"It's rare . . ."

Philo shook his head.

"Well, if you change your mind, the table is in the room to your right."

Philo nodded absently at the girl. She smiled and left.

"And now," the emcee adjusted the mike, "we have a special treat for ya'll. One of our own has just returned from a successful stint on the West Coast. Some of you already know her, and the rest of ya ain't ever gonna forget her. Ladies and gents, Lynne Halsey-Taylor!"

Cheers and whistling accompanied Lynne Halsey-Taylor to the stage. Philo felt his stomach turn over. She was dressed in the white outfit he'd bought her. She looked as

174

beautiful as she did the first time he saw her. He leaned forward in his seat, taking her in. She smiled at the crowd. Philo felt a tightness in his chest. No doubt about it, the girl affected him like nobody ever had. He closed his eyes for a moment, feeling the softness of her arms and the taste of her lips. He shivered and opened his eyes, feeling the ache in his gut for the want of her. She held up her hand.

"Thank you, Mel." Lynne turned the keys on her guitar as she talked, tuning the instrument. "Mel told you that I just came back from where Harlan is goin'. Hollywood. I gotta tell ya . . ." She gave the E string a twang, "I do just like these strings do when I come home . . . I loosen up."

The crowd laughed and applauded.

Philo listened to her voice, catching the slight inflections; a word, a phrase. He could hear her whispering in his ear.

"That should about do it." Lynne looked around the room, her face growing serious. "This here's an old Edy Lynne tune my daddy used to sing to me when I was little . . ." She began, carrying Philo back to the Palomino and all the nights and days since. The soft melody pulled at him. He swallowed. Jesus . . . He drank her in, conscious only of her, feeling her song deep inside a secret place.

Lynne finished and smiled. Applause, more whistles and cheers. She bowed and stepped off the stage, moving quickly to the rear of the club.

The emcee reappeared, clapping energetically. "Ain't she somethin'? We'll try to get Lynne to sing another for us after the next set of HOSSFAT!" He waved his arm expansively and Hossfat ran onto the stage, taking their places, grabbing their axes, and bursting into song.

Philo dropped a bill on the table and moved through the crowd to the door that opened backstage. He saw Lynne. She was smiling, looking up into the face of Nashville's own, Harlan Toothacker. Philo stopped short. When they walked into the alley that led to the parking lot, Philo followed.

Philo could see Lynne move her hip against the lanky

Toothacker. He felt a twinge in his belly. They stopped. Lynne was talking. He moved closer. Philo stepped into the shadows.

"Probably the best club out there is the Palomino, and Jimmy, the manager, is a good friend." She touched Harlan's hand. "I'll write and tell him to give you a good spot."

"Well," Harlan looked at her, smiling, placing his hand on top of hers, "that's mighty sweet of you."

Lynne smiled back, demurely. "I can't imagine how somebody who can look and sing like you do won't be a big star someday."

Harlan, a Gary Cooper. He was eating it up. Philo was beginning to feel sick.

"I really mean that." Lynne continued. "I seen a lot a guys out there. And I'd say you're almost . . . almost . . ."

Harlan reached out and took her in his arms, kissing her. Lynne threw her arms around Toothacker's neck, kissing him fiercely, pressing her body into his.

Philo watched, stunned. Pole-axed, he leaned against the wall for support.

Harlan kissed Lynne again, running his hand down her back, finding her ass, and pressing her into him.

She pulled her mouth away. "Want me?" she teased.

"Let's go," said Harlan. He grabbed her arm. She led him toward the parking lot, stopping to kiss him again. She ran her hand up his Levi's. "Harlan?"

"Yuh." The rangy Tennessean looked at her, still holding her, impatient.

Lynne hesitated. "I have a friend."

Harlan paused, unsure what she was driving at.

"Oh no, he don't mind." Lynne kissed Harlan again, leaning her body into him. "It's just that he might want to"—she studied him—"come along."

Harlan thought that one over. He smiled. "Let's go."

As they turned to leave, Philo stepped from the shadows. Lynne looked up and saw him. She stopped short. Harlan turned, and seeing Philo, backed up a step. He looked at Lynne, then back at Philo. Something was awfully wrong. Philo looked at Lynne; for him, Harlan wasn't there. The silence screamed. Too heavy for Harlan.

"Is this your . . .?" Harlan looked at Lynne.

"No." Lynne didn't look at him.

Harlan was confused. "You want to . . . uh . . . talk to him?"

Philo stared straight at Lynne. "The lady and me have some business. I s'pect you'll excuse us."

Harlan pulled himself up to his full height. "Maybe you should excuse yourself." He bristled.

Philo slowly turned his head to look at him. For Harlan, one look was enough. Lynne came to his rescue. She turned to him.

"Look . . . uh . . . it's okay, Harlan. I won't be a minute."

"You sure?" Harlan was relieved.

Lynne nodded. Harlan backed off and turned down the alley.

Philo was silent. Lynne turned to him, her eyes flashing with anger.

"What did you follow me for?" She drew in her breath. "It's your own goddamn fault. Who asked you to follow me?"

The pain showed in Philo's eyes. "I thought . . . I thought."

Lynne lashed at him. "Thought!" She looked at him contemptuously. "If you'da thought, you mighta taken some very broad hints. I been runnin', or tryin' to run away from you since almost the first night I met you!"

The words cut Philo. He felt numb. "And what about Taos?" he asked softly.

"What about it?" Lynne was aggressive, cold, and uncaring. "I'm young and healthy. I need it like anybody else."

Philo felt a surge of rage. Used. He'd opened himself to

her, knowing it was right. She didn't share those feelings. It never occurred to him. He felt dirtied, shamed, hurt, and confused. Jesus, how could he have been so dumb? What the hell had he expected? Anything but this. She was so goddamn beautiful . . . everything . . . she was . . . she was . . . slipping away . . . Goddamn, it hurt . . . He wanted to kill her . . . hurt her . . . love her. Philo felt indescribable love, pain, and hate. He closed his eyes, fighting things that he could only vaguely understand.

"You do this all the time?" He didn't really want to know.

She let him have it again. "Sure I do it, all the time." Philo wanted to throw up. "And you and me had our time already. How come you don't know when it's time to disappear?" She didn't wait for an answer, she turned to leave. Philo reached for her shoulder.

"Take your hands off me!" She spat the words, spinning out of his reach.

"Lynne? Is everything all right?" A figure stepped out of the dark and hesitantly approached them. Philo turned at the sound of the voice.

The man was slight, perhaps five-foot-six, blond and blue-eyed; a hint of petulance in his soft, full mouth. He stopped as Philo turned.

"Oh . . ." The word fell from his lips delicately. He looked at Philo with apprehension, indecisive in the flickering neon.

"Schyler, this is the one from L.A." Lynne waved her hand in Philo's direction. "The one who's been following me. The big dumb one I told you about." Schyler said nothing, his eyes wide.

Philo looked at Lynne, incredulous. "Schyler . . . with the shotgun?"

She turned to him vindictively, eyes flashing. "That was *my* idea. You were stickin' like fly-paper, and I wasn't ready to leave L.A. yet. I was hopin' it would scare you off."

"Why didn't you just say good-bye?" said Philo. His voice was tired.

"Shit!" Lynn's voice grated in the dim light. "You're here, ain't ya? Guys like you don't understand good-bye."

Confused and aware of a great weariness, Philo blurted, "You hustle for him?"

It was as though he'd slapped her face. Her shoulders slumped. The tears welled in her eyes.

Philo searched her face. "How come you never tried . . .?"

Lynne interrupted him, a deep anger smoldering. "You . . .? You were a mistake. All bull and balls. I don't usually make mistakes." She looked at the ground, then started to speak.

Philo raised his hand. "Don't . . ."

Lynne caught her breath. Then, hysterically flared. "Don't! . . . Don't what?! Don't *you* understand? You're just not too smart. You couldn't just quit like everybody else." She was almost sobbing. "Why did you have to come chasin' me and ruin it?" She wiped at her eyes angrily.

"Cause I'm not too smart, I guess," said Philo, sadly. "Cause up t' now, nobody was ever dumb enough to want to chase you farther 'n' your bed."

His words jabbed at her, each one a blow. She hated him for his gentleness, his love, and for being something more. She hated him for showing her a glimpse of something she could never be. She struck. Again and again her fists smashed into his face. She slugged him, hard, like a man. He could taste the blood. Her nails raked him.

Philo blinked but made no move to stop her. She hit him, below the eye, cutting the flesh. She beat on him, shouting. Her white satin blouse tore, bloodied.

"I hate you . . . hate . . ." His lip split. "You . . ." He stood there. "I hate . . . you . . ." Each word was punctuated by a blow. Finally her arms grew so tired she could no longer strike. They hung loosely at her side; her breath came in great gasps; her eyes vacant and staring.

Cut and bleeding, Philo observed Lynne from a great distance — a being from another planet. Then, slowly, he

179

turned and headed at Schlyer. Schyler stood terrified, afraid to stay and afraid to move. His lower lip trembled like a child's. He burst into tears.

Without a glance Philo walked past him, out of the parking lot, and into the neon night.

FOURTEEN

Orville was at the wheel, his arm around Echo. Feasted and full of fine music, it had been a good evening. A block from the motel Orville braked for the figure crossing the street in front of him. It was Philo. Orville winked at Echo and rolled down the window, a grin creasing his face from ear to ear. He pulled alongside and leaned out of the cab. Philo turned.

"Jesus Christ!" Orville's hands tightened on the wheel.

Philo's face was a mass of blood and bruises. Without a word he climbed into the driver's seat. Orville scooted over.

Orville looked at his friend. The set of Philo's jaw and the hard eyes told it all.

Orville started to say something, then changed his mind. Echo squeezed his arm. They drove on in silence. Finally Philo spoke.

"We all set?"

Orville nodded.

"How much?"

"They won't go for less than a thousand," said Orville.

"That's fine."

"You want to rest some?" said Orville tentatively. "I mean, we don't have to take him tonight."

Philo tried to smile, then winced as the effort opened his

split lip. "Orville," he said, "it's gonna be all right."

They drove on, Orville consulting a scrap of paper. He peered at the street signs. "Take a right here on Speer."

Philo turned the wheel, cutting the corner smoothly.

"Two more blocks, then left."

Philo drove on, finally turning onto a dimly lit street. Huge brick ovens, their chimneys jutting forty feet high into the air, squatted like gigantic beehives behind the fences of the Denver Brick & Pipe Company.

"This is it," said Orville.

Philo pulled into the lot. Several dozen cars were already parked. Farther ahead crouched the ovens, their 2,200-degree furnaces blazing white hot, casting an eerie orange glow, silhouetting the pyramids of brick against the Denver sky.

Philo was silent, preoccupied with his thoughts. He released Clyde from the camper and the four walked into the brickyard. Clyde, picking up Philo's feelings, was subdued. He rolled beside Philo in his peculiar gait. Perhaps a hundred people were gathered near stacks of cooling bricks on the far side of the yard. Their faces shone in the flickering golden glow. The whole scene looked surreal, moonlike. The white-hot light from the furnaces made shadows dance over huge sand dunes, clay tailings, and the silent piles of brick and pipe stacked between the grotesque ovens. Subdued voices carried through the night air. Some of the men were playing poker on the bricks.

A man approached. He looked at Clyde dubiously, then shrugged, turning his attention to Echo. He jerked his thumb at her. "You sure you want her to come?"

"Don't you worry 'bout it none," said Orville. "Where's your man?"

They followed the man toward the group playing poker. As they approached, several pointed at Clyde, laughing. Clyde ignored them, staying close to Philo. Two or three men wandered closer to get a better look.

"Hey, Tank!" The man called at the group sitting across

184

the cleared area. A large man sat with his back to Philo. He didn't look up. Carefully he finished playing his hand, throwing down his cards with a flourish, and raking in the pot. Then he turned around.

Surprise registered on Orville's face. Philo stood silent, a sphinx.

Tank Murdoch's high-school sweater was red and white, covered with little emblems showing the sports in which he'd been a four-year letterman. The many stripes on his sleeve signified his one-time status as all-city, all-state, and once, even all-America. The numerals above the large letter E told the year of Tank Murdoch's glory: 1955.

He stood up. The East Denver High sweater was much too tight for him. Too much beer over the years. He was balding and dissipated. He chewed on a cigar. Orville stared at him openly. Was this the stuff of which legends are made?

Tank walked toward Philo, followed by some of his entourage. Tank looked him up and down. He peered into Philo's face, not unfriendly. "Looks like you been in a fight." He laughed, and his friends and followers of twenty-odd years laughed with him. He studied Philo again, shaking his head, playing to his audience. "You sure that face don't hurt ya too much to fight?" Tank laughed again.

"I ain't gonna hit you with my face," said Philo.

The big man chuckled, nodding his head. His belly bounced beneath his T-shirt. "Hey, you're funny, I like you." He looked around the crowd for approval. "Don't worry." He turned his back to Philo. "I'm gonna be easy on you. It won't last too long." He took off his sweater and handed it to a man standing behind him. He swung his arms. Though big, his muscles looked flabby and soft.

Orville pulled a roll of bills from his pocket and counted out a thousand dollars. Murdoch's man did the same.

"Okay with you if the lady holds it?" asked Orville.

Murdoch's second shrugged. The two men handed the stake to Echo.'

"Make it a quick one, Tank," came a voice from the

185

crowd. "You gotta gimme a chance t' win my money back."

Tank grinned good-naturedly, waving his hand in the air. He moved into the centre of the yard with Philo, as the crowd gathered in a circle around them.

"Where'd ya hear about Tank Murdoch, kid?" he asked.

"Out there," said Philo. "They say you're the best."

Tank nodded his head, accepting his due. "They do, huh?" He smiled. "Well, let's get to it." He turned and faced Philo. The crowd hushed. They circled each other warily. Then, with all the grace of a bear, Tank moved in. Philo went to meet him. The big man cocked his right and let fly at Philo's head. Philo ducked. The blow missed him by a foot. My God, the old man was slow! Tank aimed another one, telegraphing it from Tucson. Philo walked around it. Tank backed up, concern on his face. He bored in again, throwing a left and a right. Philo was gone. Off balance, Murdoch stumbled into Philo's right. It caught him on the jaw, rocking him back on his heels. Tank turned and jabbed with his left. Philo caught him with two quick ones to the face. Tank backed up, shaking his head. He looked worried. Philo waded in, punching quickly at the larger man's gut, slashing, then jumping back out of reach. Tank grunted, dropping his guard. Philo stepped in fast. His fist crashed against Murdoch's cheek, opening it and staggering him.

With a growl, Murdoch rushed for Philo; arms outstretched, Tank tried to grab him around the waist. Philo sidestepped, clubbing Murdoch's head. The big man dropped to his knees, arms still open. The taste of blood in his mouth. Unbelieving, Murdoch slowly staggered to his feet.

The crowd murmured. Tank hadn't landed a blow. He was being cut to pieces and there was nothing he could do about it. Philo waited for Tank to get to his feet, letting him catch his breath. The big man was breathing heavily, bleeding and furious. This had never happened before. Tank was mainly angry with himself. He hadn't been able to get a shot in. Tank knew he couldn't take this punishment

186

for long. Twenty years of being No. 1, of being the best . . . going down the tubes. He felt like crying. Christ! What would they think? What would he do?

Tank charged off the ground with a bellow, tears of frustration clouding his eyes. He swung a powerful roundhouse, which spun him full circle. Philo's fist met him coming around. He didn't feel it. He swung again, maddened with his inability to connect. Another right found him and stopped him in his tracks. He could hear the voices of the crowd, angry, not believing their eyes. The great Tank Murdoch was floundering.

"Who is that guy?" Tank heard the voices from the crowd. "He's beatin' the shit outta him. C'mon, you bum!" He'd never heard that before. Tank thrashed with both fists, catching Philo on the shoulder. The crowd roared at Tank's first contact. Philo retaliated with a combination that sent Murdoch spinning across the yard. Tank fell to one knee. "Nobody's gonna whip *this* guy, ever." The words cut Tank as Philo's blows never could. He could feel the crowd's allegiance leaving. This man, this devil, was toying with him, belittling him. No dignity! Murdoch swung again. If he was going down, he was gonna fight, goddamnit. A hard left caught him on the ear and he fell into Philo. Holding on, he tried to escape the rain of blows. Philo shoved him away roughly. Tank's eyes were nearly swollen shut. He no longer felt the pounding of Philo's fists. His body was numb. Voices came to him in a jumble of sound.

"He's gonna be the new champ."

"You see them hands, fastest I ever saw."

"This guy is the best."

"There ain't no faster'n him."

Tank caught a glimpse of Clyde. The animal was standing at the edge of the circle, his arms pumping in victory. Even a fucking monkey was laughing at him, thought Tank. Philo rolled past, slamming two more to his face. Tank could barely see. The crowd was wild now, sensing the kill. Oh those fuckers, they had all deserted.

How many times he had heard those cries for him? The money didn't matter. Now they wanted to see him fall. To watch Tank Murdoch lose. Oh those lousy bastards. Philo twisted him again, sending him into the crowd. They shoved him back into the circle. Tank weaved toward Philo and tried to grab him. Philo slid away. The crowd yelled as Philo moved in once again. Tank was no longer angry. A great sadness filled him. And a great feeling of love for this lanky stranger. Funny . . . by Christ, he was the only one here who meant anything. The crowd roared.

"That guy is the absolute best." Philo heard the words.

"He'll be No. 1 forever." Out of the corner of his eye, Philo viewed the crowd. No. 1.

Forever . . . forever . . . forever . . . The words spun in Philo's head. Forever. He looked at the puffy, ageing, aching gladiator. A warmth filled him. Their eyes met and held. Philo saw Tank's heart. And also the next ten years. The never-ending procession of challenges, the same faces, the same shouts, the same . . . again and again. The same. The crowd urged him on.

Philo saw it coming long before it left the ground. It took a superhuman effort for Tank to raise his hand, much less cross those long inches to Philo's jaw.

Philo didn't move. Tank's fist floated toward him. Philo waited. It really didn't matter.

Philo heard the stunned gasp of the crowd. Lynne Halsey-Taylor had hit him harder. The ground came up to meet him...

The crowd was shocked, then they went wild. Orville stood staring, stunned.

"He did it! He did it!" The shouts echoed through the brickyard.

"That sonofabitch got a glass jaw." An ecstatic fan pounded Tank across the back. Tank shrugged him off, furious.

"You did it!" screamed another, running up to hug Murdoch. Tank shoved him away.

Tank closed his eyes, just beginning to feel the aches. Clyde looked at the old warrior with sad eyes. Tank nodded, suddenly aware that he was very tired.

He looked down at Philo Beddoe, the man who had beaten him. Twice. Then, pushing through the crowd, the winner walked away.

Philo lay there. He didn't move. Echo worried above him. Then he looked up and caught her eye. Philo smiled . . . and he winked.

The Department of Motor Vehicles, Azusa, California, a one-man operation. The President of the United States smiled down at Ma Boggs as she stood in front of the counter for her eye test. A card covered her left eye. She squinted at the letters that wavered on the wall. In her dark wig, she didn't look a day over eighty-one.

"E . . . U . . . hummmm, jest a minute. There now," Ma blinked and adjusted the card, ". . . P?"

The clerk smiled. The old man was probably the first employee for the city of Azusa. He wore a wig that might've come from the same maker as Ma's.

"Why don't you try that one with your glasses?" he suggested.

Ma glanced at him suspiciously, then smiled. "Huh? Oh yes. Humph . . . now, why didn't I think of that?" She rummaged in her handbag, finally coming up with a pair of rimless glasses. She plunked them on her nose. She looked at the clerk shyly.

"Now," said the clerk, "let's try it again." He smoothed back his wig.

"Thank ya, I will," said Ma. She looked up at the chart and quickly rattled off a string of letters. "E, U, O, P, D, C." She looked at the clerk expectantly.

"You did it!" said the clerk. His smile was benign.

Ma pulled off the glasses and stuck them in her purse. "Course I did," she said. She looked at the man out of the corner of her eye.

189

"Now," the clerk indicated footprints painted onto the floor, "would you pleased stand over there for your photograph."

"My wha . . .?" Ma stammered.

"Your photograph," said the clerk. "To put on your licence."

"My photograph!" Ma grinned self-consciously. "My, what will they think of next?" She rummaged in her purse again. "I think I forgot my comb."

The clerk looked at her, his eyes twinkling. "Your hair looks quite lovely," he said.

Ma, the consummate woman. "Do you really think so?" she asked.

Minutes later Ma Boggs climbed into the tow truck. Gallantly the clerk held the door for her.

Ma piloted the heavy vehicle through the streets of Azusa. Occasionally she looked over at the clerk, who directed her. He smiled. She was driving beautifully. Why not? She'd been driving since before the sonsabitches was born!

Heading west through the Rockies, blue skies, sunshine, and white water. On the radio, somebody's feeling good and singing about it. Inside the Apache, cold beer and warm feelings. Orville gently nuzzled Echo as Philo hummed along with the song. Ahead of them on the highway, a black speck grew until it took shape. Battered and beaten, a resurrected '68 Cadillac limousine, its top sawed off, smoked, belched, rattled, and blew down the blacktop. Eleven Black Widows, bandaged and bloody, in no better shape than their transportation, were crammed into the decrepit machine.

A three-wheeled motorcycle, its forks resting in the trunk, trailed behind. A jackbooted figure sat majestically astride the saddle, caked in mud, wearing the classic expression of every leader of the pack.

Passing the pitiful pack at seventy, the Apache rocked with laughter.

Somewhere in New Mexico. High roads and low winds. Coming at them down the highway, a groaning tow truck, dragged one godawful-looking Jeep pickup, its every conceivable extra covered with three hundred pounds of moss, slime, and mud. Inside the cab, were two of the sorriest-looking cops in all of L.A.

As they disappeared in the rear-view, a long, loving arm reached into the cab, draping itself entirely around Philo, Orville, and Echo.

Ahead, the blacktop stretched, shimmering into the distance. Country music followed like a good friend, and like it said:

They were going home.

Wyndham Books are obtainable from many booksellers and newsagents. If you have any difficulty please send purchase price plus postage on the scale below to:

Wyndham Cash Sales
P.O. Box 11
Falmouth
Cornwall
OR
Star Book Service,
G.P.O. Box 29,
Douglas,
Isle of Man,
British Isles.

While every effort is made to keep prices low, it is sometimes necessary to increase prices at short notice. Wyndham Books reserve the right to show new retail prices on covers which may differ from those advertised in the text or elsewhere.

Postage and Packing Rate

UK: 30p for the first book, plus 15p per copy for each additional book ordered to a maximum charge of £1.29.
BFPO and Eire: 30p for the first book, plus 15p per copy for the next 6 books and thereafter 6p per book.
Overseas: 50p for the first book and 15p per copy for each additional book.

These charges are subject to Post Office charge fluctuations.